RUN TO EARTH

Free at last after their long and dangerous journey, Black Tip, Vickey and the other foxes are looking forward to cubbing time, but in the Land of Sinna the fight for survival never ends, and now a new threat hangs over the valley. Moons of death strike from the evergreens and a powerful predator swoops from the sky. The new danger menaces all the animals in the valley, large and small, but as natural enemies, will they come together to save the valley – and themselves?

RUN TO EARTH

To Tim and Kathleen Kelly, in whose locality I studied many of the things that were to become features of the Land of Sinna; to Martina Byrne for her love of animals; and to her mother, Molly.

RUN TO EARTH

by

Tom McCaughren

Dales Large Print Books
Long Preston, North Yorkshire,
BD23 4ND, England.

British Library Cataloguing in Publication Data.

McCaughren, Tom
 Run to earth.

 A catalogue record of this book is
 available from the British Library

 ISBN   978-1-84262-522-4 pbk

First published in 1999 Wolfhound Press

Text Copyright © 1983, 2005 Tom McCaughren

Cover illustration © Viney by arrangement with
P.W.A. International Ltd.

The moral right of the author has been asserted

Published in Large Print 2007 by arrangement with
Merlin Books Ltd.

Dales Large Print is an imprint of Library Magna Books Ltd.

Printed and bound in Great Britain by
T.J. (International) Ltd., Cornwall, PL28 8RW

Contents

Acknowledgements

I would like to thank a number of people who helped me in the course of my research. In particular, I greatly appreciate the help and hospitality I received from Tim and Kathleen Kelly of Luggacurren, Co Laois, when I was observing the progression of the seasons. They also provided me with much background information which was invaluable, and kindly allowed me to study the stoat hunting antics of their pets, Oscar and Felix, so that I could give a greater sense of realism to some of the animal characters I wished to portray, not only in this book, but in *Run with the Wind*. Similarly, I would like to thank Dermot and Loretto McDonnell, who gave me the run of their farm at Mortarstown, Carlow, and helped me with various aspects of my research.

I am grateful to a number of other people in the Carlow area, including my wife's mother, Mrs Molly Byrne, and sister Martina, of Mortarstown, Joan McDonnell of Cloughna, Jim Townsend of Linkardstown, and PJ and Ciss Keating of Rathoe.

My thanks also to Mrs Pattie Madden of Kilkenny Road, Carlow, for telling me the story she heard from her father about how a fox gets rid of fleas. Dr J S Fairley, in his natural history of Ireland's furred wildlife, *An Irish Beast Book*, relates how a forestry worker once told him a similar story. He says he is still sceptical, and indeed some wildlife experts say it doesn't happen. But who knows?

I would like to place on record my thanks to Don Conroy, the wildlife artist, for kindly introducing me to his birds of prey; the late Detective Chief Superintendent Dan Murphy, for allowing me to take a phrase or two from his reminiscences, and adapt them to this story; Joe and Monica Moorehouse of Healy's Bridge, Carrigrohane, Co. Cork, for allowing me to study their pet fox; and Jim Norton, who at the time of writing was President of the Wicklow Sheep Owners' Association and of the Wicklow Mountain Sheep Breeder's Society.

I am also grateful for the assistance I received from Liam O'Flanagan, Forestry and Wildlife Service, Department of Fisheries and Forestry, and Aidan Brady, former Director of the National Botanic Gardens, Dublin.

In addition, I would like to thank the staff of the National Library of Ireland for giving me access to copies of the Dublin Evening

Mail of January, 1839, so that I could study contemporary accounts of the Night of the Big Wind.

I would also like to thank Mary Paul Keane, who was a great help to me while she was Production Editor of Wolfhound Press, and Aoife Barrett, Editorial Manager at Merlin Publishing.

Last, but not least, I wish to thank once again my wife Fran for her unstinting support and seemingly unending patience; as well as my daughters, Michelle, Amanda, Samantha and Simone.

In conclusion, I might point out that the farmers mentioned here may not agree with my view of the fox, but that did not prevent them from helping me when I asked them.

TOM MCCAUGHREN
2005

ONE

The Wind of Change

The last streaks of snow had faded from the mountain, and the wind that blew down the mountainside was beginning to lose its bite. It ruffled the calm waters of the lake and fanned the reeds so that they looked like great goose quills lodged in the mud. It brushed the slender branches of the pussy willows and waved the new-grown grass as it made its way across the meadows. It rustled the withered leaves, still matted beneath the balding bulrushes, and caressed the newly-budding blackthorn bushes up by the back of Beech Paw. It tickled the catkins on the hazel bushes and gently swayed the spruce trees up in the evergreens so that they nodded like giant ferns.

On the rim of the quarry, a vixen lay and looked out across the valley. The wind flicked her fur this way and that, and while it wasn't yet warm, she knew that it breathed new life as it passed. Somehow she felt part of it, for she too had breathed new life into the valley and into her own species at a time when it needed it most. She turned

13

her head and her left ear twitched as it caught the sound of whimpering from the den below. Her two cubs were stirring and searching the darkness for the warm belly that gave them life.

The vixen, known in the fox world as Vickey, smiled to herself. The cubs could wait, she thought. In the distance she could see two other foxes. They were under the tall willow at the edge of the lake, and she knew one was Black Tip, her mate. She also knew that he would look after her needs first, then his own. Behind her, somewhere up among the blackthorns, three thrushes played out their own mating game on the bare branches of a spindle tree. Like the other birds of the hedgerows, they needed only the cover of green leaves before building a home. Then, she thought, they would all have more cover and life would be easier for everyone.

Vickey's ears twitched again, this time to the sound of man's machines farther down the valley. Man was always changing things, she thought. Always cutting. If it wasn't the trees or the very hedgerows themselves, it was the meadow grass. And if he wasn't doing that he was draining the meadows and dredging the streams. Man never seemed to realise that his work always meant leaner times and sometimes death for the creatures of the countryside. But at least his sounds were now far enough distant not to worry her.

Much more pleasant was the cawing of the crows, she thought. As part of a twig dropped beside her she looked up to see the dark silhouette of a rook winging its way across the fields to the long row of beech trees that stretched up from the meadows. She smiled again. The crows were busy building their nests in the topmost branches. No need for them to wait. The branches were bare and would be bare for some time to come. But it made no difference to them. As with the magpies, the leaves, when they came, would give them privacy; protection was something they could provide for themselves.

The whimpering from the den was becoming more urgent now, so Vickey eased herself up. With another glance around to make sure no danger approached, she turned and made her way down through the new dock leaves and under the brambles to the den beneath the overhanging rocks where her cubs waited to be fed. And then, as they found her teats and she curled her brush around them to give them warmth and comfort, there was a contented silence in the quarry, a silence that not even the crows or man's machines could break.

Black Tip picked his way across the meadows. He was in high spirits and there

15

was a spring in his step, for everywhere about him were signs that after a long hard winter the valley was coming back to life. Beneath him he could feel the softness of new grass and the sponginess of meadow moss. He threw a glance up towards the nesting crows and knew that everything at Beech Paw was normal. Then he followed the fox path up the side of the valley until he came to an ash tree from which a storm or perhaps a snowfall had shorn a lower branch. The base of the branch still clung to the trunk with enough bark to feed its twigs even though they now rested on the ground. Thus the branch arched the fox path to form a place where foxes might pause, leave scents and tell others where and when they had passed.

Several great tits who were sporting themselves in the uppermost branches of the tree flew off into the hedgerows at Black Tip's approach, but he barely gave them a glance. Instead he dropped the dead rat he was carrying and lay down in the withered grass that had grown up to meet the tips of the fallen branch.

The buds on the ash, he could see, were still black and hard; he knew that, as with the beech, it would take more than a softening of the wind to prize them open. However, other trees and bushes had not been so slow. Man might not have noticed, for he can walk through the countryside and see little, but every bud and flower, every scent and sound, are as important to the creatures who live there as life itself. They miss very little and so, while nature must remind man of the changing season by a bold splash of pink of the cherry trees, the creatures of the wild see more subtle changes, changes as quiet and unobtrusive as themselves.

First it was the elder. Black Tip's sharp eye had spotted short strokes of green on the grey bark and found fresh leaves sprouting from soft shoots that man might have taken for dead. They had slipped out in tight little bunches at a time when nothing was to be seen on the hawthorn but blue tufts of lichen and a smattering of weather-beaten haws that had blackened and shrivelled in the cold of winter. Then, even while the mountain slopes beyond the lake were still a tangled mass of brown, hardier ferns had spread like stars along the streams and ditches. Now it seemed the whole valley was getting ready to green, and knowing the new life it would bring, Black Tip was glad. Picking up the rat, he watered the black unyielding ash buds. If they refused to come out, he smiled, at least they could carry his mark!

Making his way up towards Beech Paw, Black Tip paused once more, this time to savour the scents on a large flat stone where small birds had plucked at the moss in search of insects and tiny worms. But the birds had gone now. He was wasting his time, so he squeezed through a hawthorn hedge where it gave way to a large chestnut tree and trotted up along the dry ditch beneath the beeches and the nesting crows. Then he cut across the fields to the quarry.

The cubs were full and fast asleep in the cradle of Vickey's brush, and Vickey herself was dozing when she became aware of the movement outside. Pausing briefly so that her eyes could adjust to the light, she greeted Black Tip with a customary rubbing of noses, and sniffed the rat he had brought her. Then she went back into the den and Black Tip followed. In the darkness of the den the amber of their eyes parted as their pupils opened wide to take in all available light.

Black Tip looked at the cubs with pride. 'They're getting bigger every day,' he remarked.

Vickey nodded and, referring to the one with a slight suggestion of black on the end of its tail, said, 'Little Black Tip's going to be a strong dog.'

'Like me,' smiled Black Tip, thinking of the day he had fought a fox called Fang in the hollow below the quarry to win Vickey for his mate.

Vickey felt like saying that at the end of the

day perhaps their real strength lay in the vixen who produced the cubs, but she refrained from doing so, for she knew that until the cubs were weaned and her own body became strong again, they must depend on the strength of the dog fox. Furthermore, it was she herself who had said to Black Tip that foxes must share their strength – and their cunning – if they were to survive at a time when there were so few of them left. Anyway, Black Tip was a strong fox. It was he who had led them in a search for the secret of survival, and in her heart she knew he would be the first to speak of her strength too, the strength of spirit that had brought them back to Beech Paw. So she just licked the other cub affectionately and said, 'What do you think of little Running Fox?'

'She's beautiful,' he said. 'How could she be anything else.'

Vickey was glad now that she hadn't rebuked Black Tip and inwardly rebuked herself for having such quarrelsome thoughts. Yet she knew she wasn't really to blame. Cubbing could have an unsettling effect on vixens and she was no exception.

'Who was the other fox I saw at the lake?' she asked.

'Ratwiddle,' Black Tip told her.

'Poor Ratwiddle,' said Vickey. 'He'll kill himself yet.'

'If the rats don't kill him first.'

Vickey nodded. 'I know.' She went outside and buried the rat in one of the many places she kept food. 'I'll eat it later,' she said.

'Well, it's there when you want it,' said Black Tip, but he knew what she was thinking. Ratwiddle had always been a worry to her.

Curling herself around the cubs, Vickey began to tell them softly about a wise old fox, a friend of theirs called Old Sage Brush.

Black Tip wondered if the cubs could hear her, for it seemed to him that they had gone to sleep again.

'It doesn't matter,' Vickey told him. 'Hasn't Old Sage Brush shown us that our eyes can be open but still be blind, our ears open but still be deaf?'

Black Tip knew this to be true, for on their search for the secret of survival it had often appeared that they were the ones who were blind, not Old Sage Brush. At the same time he wondered: 'What has that got to do with it?'

'It's just that I feel the sound of my voice gives them comfort,' Vickey told him. 'And who's to know what they can hear in their sleep?'

Black Tip knew he couldn't argue with the logic of a vixen's love for her cubs, strange as it might be, so he listened as she quietly recounted a story that the old fox had told them.

It was the story of how the fox god Vulpes, realising that some day his species would face extinction, had caused a great wind to blow. It had torn up the trees and ripped open the land and had taken the mountains and reshaped them to form their valley. And then, she told them, he had put a great white fox to rule over it and entrusted him with the secret of survival.

Vickey went on to recall that even though he was blind, Old Sage Brush had agreed to help them try and find that secret, and how they had set off with a few others: Fang who had lost the fight with Black Tip but become his friend, Hop-along who had only three legs, another vixen called She-la, and Skulking Dog who had joined them along the way.

'When you're old enough to look up,' she whispered to her cubs, 'you'll see a great running fox twinkling in the sky, and he will guide you on your journeys through life, just as he guided us as we journeyed in search of the secret of survival.'

'And don't forget to tell them how Skulking Dog rescued the old fox's daughter Sinnéad from the howling dogs,' said Black Tip. 'And about the great fight we had with the fun dogs. They didn't think it was much fun chasing foxes when we had finished with them.'

'Don't worry,' Vickey assured him, 'I won't.' Then she told him something that

21

not even he was aware of. 'I never told you before,' she said, 'but the fight with the fun dogs cost us the life of one of our cubs.'

Black Tip looked up, surprised. 'I didn't know,' he said quietly, and he wondered how she knew, for as with rabbits and field mice and many other mammals, fox-cubs that die before birth are reabsorbed into their mother's body.

'Don't ask me how I know,' she added, 'I just know. Otherwise we would have had three.'

'But if you and the other vixens hadn't come to our aid we'd all have been killed,' Black Tip reminded her. 'And then we'd have no cubs, for we'd all be dead.'

Vickey nodded. 'I know that, but I just thought I should tell you.'

Black Tip smiled. 'You'll have to tell them about the other foxes who helped us along the way. And about Whiskers the otter. He was a great help to us.'

'There's so much to tell them,' said Vickey. 'And we must teach them all the things we've learned from Old Sage Brush, all the secrets that will help them survive.' She licked her cubs affectionately and suggested: 'Why don't you check to see how Hop-along and She-la are getting on. I worry about them.'

Black Tip got up to go. 'They're well placed up in the blackthorns. But you've reason to worry. She-la's coming near her time and Hop-along will find it hard to forage for all of them with only three legs.'

'Well, see what you can do for them. And maybe then you can look in on Sinnéad and Skulking Dog.'

'I will,' Black Tip assured her. 'And keep an eye out for Ratwiddle. He said he might call.' He paused on the way out. 'Oh, and one more thing. You better make Ratwiddle keep his distance. He's got fleas.'

TWO

Ratwiddle

On the far side of the valley, the sharp eyes of another predator scanned the meadows. A peregrine falcon took off from a disused ravens' nest on the rocky slope above the lake and circled the Mountain of Vulpes. No movement, however small, escaped his notice, and he saw Black Tip slipping out of the quarry. However, the falcon was gliding around in search of food and, with barely a glance at the fox, winged his way up the valley towards the heathered slopes which he knew contained a covey of red grouse.

Caution dictated that Black Tip should not go direct to Hop-along's earth. Experience had shown him that it was always safer to circle around in case man or dog might try to follow. So he made his way down from the quarry to the hollow where he had fought Fang. Spring had long since released the stream from its icy grip and it now sparkled and gurgled its way freely down the hillside. As it did so it also irrigated the hollow, so that it had become an oasis of green among the barren fields of Beech

Paw. Dark green clumps of hogweed leaves had sprung up around the dry grey stalks of last year's flowers, the grass had become light green and lush, a lushness that even the meadow grass had yet to acquire, while humps of rushes had taken on a firmer and richer sheen of their own.

Black Tip paused to lap the cool refreshing water of the stream, recalling as he did so how the same water had helped to heal their wounds and bring Fang back to life the day they had met and fought for Vickey. He wondered where Fang was now, but had no way of knowing. Then, turning his thoughts once more to Hop-along, he made his way up along the stream, knowing that the water would sweep away his scent, and circled around towards the belt of scrub that ran across the hillside below the evergreens.

On the brow of the hill he came across the partly-eaten carcass of a wood pigeon and, judging by the amount of downy feathers scattered around it, guessed that it had been killed by a hunting bird. He looked up and scanned the sky for the fluttering wings, and seeing none, picked up the remains of the bird and took it with him. The three thrushes were still playing a game of hide-and-seek in among the spindle trees, but at his approach took off and flew down to the horse chestnut beyond the beeches.

He found Hop-along's earth in under a

patch of low blackthorn scrub. It was well concealed and protected by the sturdy thorns, and it was only with difficulty that he got to the entrance. Hop-along had chosen well. With his handicap, he needed all the protection nature could provide, and in a short time it would provide even more. Clusters of leaves had already emerged from the tangles of honeysuckle vines which only a short time earlier had all the appearance of having withered in winter, while masses of small pink buds would blossom to give the blackthorns a covering of white even before they came into leaf.

There was no sign of Hop-along, or of his mate She-la, so Black Tip left the pigeon for them and made his way up to the entrance at the back. To his surprise, he found that they had blocked it by pulling a blackthorn shrub into it and not wishing to interfere with whatever they had been doing, he went out the front and made his way beneath the scrub.

Sensing the presence of a fox in the blackthorns, a blackbird gave a clattering cry of alarm and flapped noisily through the bushes, coming to rest a short distance away with a few more protesting clucks. Pausing briefly, Black Tip listened for any sign that it might have alerted man or any other creature to his presence, then satisfied that it hadn't, he thought how he disliked the blackbird for making such a rumpus. As a passing thought he wondered if it had started to build its nest. In general, he knew, the hedgerow birds hadn't started building yet, but with the blackbird he couldn't be sure. While it exposed everyone else's movements, it was very secretive about its own.

Emerging from the blackthorns, Black Tip hurried up over the hill towards the evergreens. There he turned to scan the valley. Beyond the lake the Mountain of Vulpes was cloaked in the foxy brown of last year's ferns. High above the lake, on the edge of the steep rocky slope the familiar figure of a white billy-goat stood motionless, a silent sentinel whose very presence for many years had kept the mountain sheep from falling to their deaths. The sheep had been brought down from the mountain now and he could see them gathered in the fields around the farm buildings where they could lamb in safety and shelter if the frosty nights returned.

Hoping he might find Hop-along in the evergreens, he crossed over a low stone wall beneath a line of hazel bushes. The hazels were festooned with golden brown catkins that hung from the twigs like lambs' tails. And in the plantation beyond, the larch trees were smudged with spots of red as new cones the size of raspberries spread along branches which were becoming greener and more graceful with each day of spring. However, on the ground beneath, the dry needles of springs gone by yielded neither the scent nor the signs Black Tip was looking for, so he doubled back down to the blackthorns and followed them along until he came to the beech trees.

In the fields beyond, Black Tip was squeezing through beneath a hawthorn hedge when he was shocked to see another fox struggling in the hedgerow opposite. It was Hop-along! His first impulse was to rush to his assistance, but some instinct stopped him. Reading the signs, he noted that Hop-along's left front leg was caught in a thin copper wire tied to a stake that was driven into the soil at the entrance to a rabbit burrow. A short distance away, a number of rabbits were nibbling the grass, quite unconcerned with his presence. Black Tip eased himself down and watched. Hop-along also lay down and watched the rabbits. After a while one, lulled into a false sense of security, ventured closer, and it didn't notice what Black Tip noticed. Casually Hop-along turned his head away as if he was curling up to go asleep. Instead, he gripped the short wooden stake with his teeth and drew it out of the soil. In the same instant he sprang to life and seized the unsuspecting rabbit. A moment later there was no one in the field but the two foxes.

Black Tip smiled. 'I can see the lessons we

learned from Old Sage Brush haven't gone to waste.'

Hop-along hobbled over to meet him, and let Black Tip help him take the copper wire off his leg. 'When you've lost a leg you've got to make more use of your head.'

'The old fox couldn't have put it better,' said Black Tip. 'But I thought you would have been afraid to put your leg in a choking hedge trap after what happened before.'

'This is just a small one man had put down for rabbits,' said Hop-along. 'Anyway, it wasn't a choking hedge trap that caught me before. It was the snapping jaws. Once they catch you, there's no way they'll let you go. That's why I had to chew my leg off.'

Black Tip could see that Hop-along was looking lean and under-fed. He knew, of course, that all dog foxes lose weight during cubbing time as they have to hunt for their vixens as well as themselves, and that this must be particularly difficult for a fox with only three legs. 'How long have you been waiting for the rabbits to come close?' he asked.

'Long enough,' replied Hop-along. He smiled. 'But I got one, a good one, and that's what matters.' Then he added in a more serious tone: 'Anyway, that's the least of my worries...'

'Why, what else worries you? Is She-la all right?'

'She's fine. But there's no sign of her cubs yet, and she's become very moody. She keeps going off on her own and I can't hunt and keep an eye on her at the same time.'

Black Tip nodded. He knew well how moody a vixen could become as her cubbing time approached.

They were trotting through the beeches now and as they paused to admire a red squirrel streaking from one tree to another on its way back up to the evergreens, Black Tip asked: 'Is there anything else?'

Hop-along dropped the rabbit. 'I haven't said anything to She-la about it, but during the past night or two when I was out hunting, I got the smell of cat.'

'Cat?' said Black Tip. 'Why worry about a cat?'

'Because I think there must be more than one. The rabbits have gone scared. That's why it's taking me twice as long to catch them. So they must be after them too.'

'Is that why you've blocked the back entrance to your earth with blackthorns?'

Hop-along nodded. 'Nothing can get in, but if need be we can push it out and escape when the time comes.'

'What time?' asked Black Tip.

'Cubbing time.'

'But you don't think they'd...?'

'When you're like me,' said Hop-along, 'you have to think of everything.'

As they trotted back to Hop-along's earth, Black Tip thought about the cats. Had they come up from the farms, he wondered, or were they living wild? And while he didn't say so, he felt Hop-along might well have cause to worry, especially if they were cats that had gone wild. For while the fox is related to the dog, it is more feline in its ways and will give way to a cat rather than fight it. That's not to say, however, that a fox won't fight a cat. Black Tip had fought one once, a wild one, and killed it, but he had found it an agile and difficult adversary. Ever since he had had a healthy respect for them, and preferred if they went their separate ways. Hop-along's fears, of course, might be due more to his handicap than to any real threat. Nevertheless, he told himself he must mention it to Vickey, just in case.

When Black Tip arrived back at the quarry, he saw Ratwiddle sitting outside the den. He smiled. He knew Vickey was making him keep his distance because of his fleas. While he was amused, he also knew she had good reason for making him stay outside, for she had told him she had once seen a weak cub dying after it had been infested with lice. Consequently, he decided to stay outside too, in case Ratwiddle might follow him in.

Ratwiddle had got his name from the fact that the other foxes believed his brain had been addled from hunting rats down by the lake. Old Sage Brush had told them that while they could eat rats without any problem, they should be careful, as they could take sick and die if rats' water got into a cut or sore. They assumed it was this sickness that had done something strange to Ratwiddle's brain. He seldom mixed with other foxes and had never mated. Instead, he spent most of his time searching among the gnarled roots of the willows as if his sole purpose in life was to seek out and destroy all the rats in the lake. It was the same sickness, they knew, that had also left him with a stiff neck, a peculiarity that was emphasised by the fact that he wore a red dog collar. How the collar had come to be on his neck not even he could explain, but it didn't seem to bother him. He just trotted around with his head twisted sideways and his nose in the air in a way that suggested his mind was on more important things.

Now as Black Tip lay down beside him he twisted his neck even further so that his right eye looked skywards and scratched himself vigorously.

'You should take those fleas for a swim,' remarked Vickey from inside the den.

'That's right,' said Black Tip. 'I think it's time you pulled the wool over their eyes.'

Ratwiddle stopped scratching and shook his head. 'No, not the wool.'

'But Ratwiddle,' insisted Vickey, 'Old Sage Brush says the flea that dares to bite the fox must be allowed to drink its fill.'

'I know,' Ratwiddle replied, 'but I cannot. It's the rats you see. They're waiting to drag me down. That's why I must kill them. All of them.' He continued to scratch himself and stare stiff-necked at the sky.

'Are you still having the same dream?' Black Tip asked him.

'It's the water,' he told them 'It's rising.'

'Rising?' exclaimed Vickey, getting to her feet and coming to the mouth of the den.

'So you *are* still having your dream,' said Black Tip.

'It's rising,' continued Ratwiddle. 'It's always the same. It's rising, and the rats are dragging me down. They're pulling the wool over my eyes and I can't see. I must kill them before they drag me down.'

'We know a fox who had a dream like that once,' said Vickey soothingly. 'His name's Hop-along, and he has only three legs. He dreamt that the mountain hares were dragging him down, but he found a way of outjumping them. Maybe he could help you Ratwiddle – you know, tell you what your dream means – and then you won't be afraid of it any more.'

'No,' said Ratwiddle slowly.

'Why not?' asked Black Tip.

'Because the only way he can look into my

33

dreams is to look into my head.'

'And what's wrong with that?' asked Vickey.

'He'd just be wasting his time.'

'How do you know?' asked Black Tip.

'Because I just know,' replied Ratwiddle slowly. 'You see, he'd be like a blind fox in a dark earth, looking for a black cat that's not there.'

Perplexed by Ratwiddle's strange reply, Vickey felt for a moment as if it was her brain that was addled, not his, but she just said, 'We know a blind fox, and he can see farther than most. He's been a great help to us. Maybe he can help you.'

Ratwiddle, however, continued to stare at the sky, and it was obvious his mind was beyond their reach.

'That reminds me,' said Black Tip, 'Hopalong says he has got the scent of cats up in the evergreens.'

'What colour?' asked Vickey, and Black Tip knew she was thinking of an incident in which she had been run to earth by a big black-and-tan cat and a terrier. It had happened just before she had given birth to her cubs.

'All cats look black in the dark,' remarked Ratwiddle and getting up, he trotted stiff-necked out of the quarry and disappeared.

In some strange way, Vickey found Ratwiddle's remarks unnerving. 'What does he mean?' she asked irritably.

'I don't know,' confessed Black Tip. 'I just mentioned the cats so that we should be on the alert, that's all.' So saying, he leaned back and began to scratch himself.

'Well, he's left you some of his fleas,' said Vickey. 'Better get rid of them. But before you do Black Tip, would you go down as far as the fox tails and check the water for me?'

Black Tip sighed. There seemed no end to a vixen's anxieties at cubbing time. However, he knew he must be patient with her, so he smiled and assured her, 'Of course it's not rising. It's the rats' water that's rising in Ratwiddle's brain, that's all. You know that.'

THREE

Chasing Shadows

Because of what Hop-along had said about the cats, Black Tip didn't stray far from the quarry that night. He hunted in the fields nearby, and when he returned he decided to lie up on the rim of the quarry, partly because Vickey wouldn't let him into the den as long as he had fleas, but also because he wanted to keep an eye out for any danger.

By morning he realised he had picked up quite a few fleas from Ratwiddle and, finding that the scratching was beginning to inflame his skin, he decide to take Vickey's advice and do what all healthy foxes should do to fleas: pull the wool over their eyes. First though, he had promised Vickey he would go down to the lake and make sure there was nothing in what Ratwiddle had said. So, having circled widely and found no scent of danger, he made his way down to a clump of reeds, which they called fox tails, that grew by the water's edge.

Known to man as the common reed, these particular reeds are held in very high esteem by foxes, for they're bushy and brown like their own tails and on close examination even display in inner greyness not unlike the colour of their own fur when it's flicked aside by the wind.

Concealing himself among the withered leaves, Black Tip looked at the Mountain of Vulpes. The wind from the mountain caused a gentle rustling in the brittle cane-like stems above him, and as it did so, it brought him the strong smell of sheep and possibly mountain hare. The lake, he was not surprised to see, was at the level it always was, as everlasting and unchanging as the mountain itself. As he looked across at the mountain now, he wondered what Old Sage Brush had meant by his story about the great god Vulpes. What was it the old fox had told them? The fox god in his wisdom, he had said, had realised that one day the fox would face extinction, so he had caused a great wind to blow and reshape the mountains and form the Land of Sinna, a valley where they could survive and so perpetuate their species. But what did he mean? Foxlore did speak of a time when man in the valley had respected the fox; but no more, and he wondered why.

A sudden fluttering on the surface of the water brought him back to reality. A pair of mallard ducks were swimming out near a small wooded island in the middle of the lake, and they reminded him that he must hunt. First, however, he must rid himself of his fleas, otherwise Vickey wouldn't let him near the cubs.

Raising his head, his large black ears turned this way and that as they read the sounds of the valley. From the farm at the lower end of the lake came the distant bleating of new-born lambs. However, he realised it would be foolhardy to go there for the wool he needed. The farmer would almost certainly think he was after the lambs and he couldn't risk drawing danger on to his own new-born. Safer, he thought, to try the mountain slopes.

Taking off at a fast trot along the lake shore, Black Tip paused momentarily to sniff at a yellow flower man calls coltsfoot, but which foxes see as an early dandelion and another sign of better times to come. It had been watered by Ratwiddle. Not wishing to take on board any more fleas, he avoided the willows where Ratwiddle hunted and made a wide sweep around the lake until he came to the river at the upper end of the lake. The banks were lined with alder, hazel and an assortment of sallows, and he stopped to check a field in a secluded bend which he knew was sometimes used by sparring pheasants. The signs suggested that it wasn't so long since a pair of cocks had been fighting there, so he decided he would pay another visit to the field soon.

Crossing the river, he made his way over the meadows and climbed up through the heather on the far slopes. Since the sheep had been taken down for lambing, he was able to move around without creating a stir. Here and there he saw small tufts of wool clinging to branches of hawthorn and brambles and occasionally a few hairs that had got snagged on a knotted piece of sheep wire. But he needed something more substantial, so he climbed higher until he came to a spot where a piece of barbed wire had been twisted up out of harm's way. It was intertwined with a heavy briar, and between them the barbs and thorns had pulled a large portion of wool from the back of some unfortunate sheep. Reaching up, he closed his teeth on a good mouthful of it and pulled. It came away quite easily, and he turned and went back to the reeds on the far side of the lake. Ratwiddle was sitting in the grass scratching himself, but when Black Tip offered him some of the wool, he just ignored him and carried on scratching.

Having satisfied himself that there was no danger in the vicinity, Black Tip went down to the edge of the water, turned and slowly backed in. He could feel the water creeping up his legs, then up his hind quarters and his belly. He paused. He could also feel the fleas moving through his fur ahead of the water. Slowly he backed in farther, then a little farther. The water was almost over his back now and he felt the fleas climbing up over his head. Gently he lowered himself under the water until only his snout and the wool were above the surface. Then, when the fleas had taken their last jump and abandoned him for the mouthful of wool, he opened his jaws and let them float off. Coming to the surface, he watched with a smile as the wool became soaked and sank, taking his tormentors with it.

While this strange ritual was going on, Ratwiddle had stopped scratching to watch. But even before Black Tip had finished shaking the water from his coat, he was trotting away, stiff-necked along the shore, almost as if he had a flea in his ear. Black Tip shook his head. Poor Ratwiddle, he thought. If the rats didn't kill him, the fleas most surely would.

Free now himself of fleas, Black Tip spent the rest of the day with his cubs. As they slept, he lay and admired them and talked to Vickey about how she had named the little vixen after the Great Running Fox in the Sky. 'It will be a great friend to them,' he whispered, 'once they know how to follow it.'

Vickey nodded. 'I hope it will always be there when they need it. I don't want them to take any wrong turns.'

'Don't worry, they won't,' Black Tip assured her, and he closed his eyes and recalled how Old Sage Brush had taught them to follow the formation of stars that man calls the Plough, but which foxes see as shaped in their own image and thus call the Great Running Fox in the Sky.

'Don't worry,' he repeated. 'The great god Vulpes will always keep it in their view.'

'But it can only help them at gloomglow,' said Vickey. 'What happens when the howling dogs come? Who will guide them then?'

'They'll be guided by us,' said Black Tip, 'and by all that we've learned.'

Vickey shivered. 'Still, it frightens me to think of the dangers that lie ahead of them.'

'Well,' said Black Tip, 'we'll just have to make sure they're ready to meet them, that's all.'

The cubs stirred to life and immediately went for their mother's teats, but she fended them off, for she knew their stomachs were still full. Instead, she licked them and nuzzled them and told them stories her mother had told her: stories of days gone by when the fields had given more cover and food had been more plentiful; when once a year had been enough for farmers to cut the grass, and hedges had hardly needed cutting at all. In those days, she whispered, long-legged birds that had craked in the grass had been a great source of food. Many of them had been killed by the flashing blades when the grass had grown so tall it had to be cut, but there had always been more of them. Then had come the day when the farmers couldn't wait for the grass to grow long. They had begun to cut it in spring when the long-legged birds were nesting, and when the flashing blades had destroyed the eggs, the long-legged birds had craked no more. After that, she added, life had become harder for them all.

The cubs were becoming restless now, searching again for their mother's teats. Small and all as the cubs were, their mouths were already large and they had drained much of the strength from her body. Without a word, she rose, dislodging them as she did so, and left the den. Black Tip knew she was going over to the circle of beeches they called Beech Paw, to rest, and he was glad. He could see the cubs were getting stronger by the day. Their ears were still rounded, but their pale blue eyes were changing colour and would soon be soft brown. Already the light was drawing them to the mouth of the den, but they were still too small to wander so he gently brought them back and played with them until Vickey returned.

They stayed together until nightfall. Then, when Vickey and the cubs were asleep, Black Tip slipped out of the quarry to hunt. It was a clear frosty night. Scents were strong and full of promise. When he had found enough food for Vickey and himself he would sleep, and in the morning he would call on Skulking Dog and Sinnéad.

Old habits die hard, even with foxes, and Skulking Dog had dug an earth near another line of beeches overlooking the farm at the lower end of the lake. During his journey with Old Sage Brush and the others, his weakness for farmyard hens had almost cost him his life. Every time he thought of it he could still feel the shotgun pellets ripping through his rump. He had been greedy, and he had been lucky. As the old fox had said, 'Hasn't Vulpes shown us that the greedy fox who snaps off many heads when one will do, will lose his own?' After that he had been careful, and now that he had four new-born cubs he had to be extra careful. His mate, Sinnéad, wouldn't have it any other way, and insisted that not even one head should be snapped off at the farm. Now was their most vulnerable time, as they were in no position to run. Skulking Dog, of course, was well aware of this and so, while he watched the hens and savoured their scent, he hunted elsewhere.

Sinnéad had cubbed early. In the normal run of things, She-la would have cubbed before her, but for some reason or other She-la's waiting time had turned out to be longer. The waiting time, as all vixens knew, was the worst. Nevertheless, Sinnéad felt sure that it would all work out well in the end and Skulking Dog would do what he could to help Hop-along with whatever other problems he had. In the meantime, she herself would be fully occupied with her own cubs, a little dog and three vixens.

Like all fathers, Skulking Dog thought the male was the image of him, while Sinnéad felt sure she could already see signs of a small white spot on the forehead of one of the vixens, a white spot just like her own.

In truth, however, as she gave them their first lick she thought how small and unfox-like they really were. Yet how she loved them and how much she knew her father, Old Sage Brush, would love them, if he could only see them. Man, of course, had ensured that he would never see them, having poked out his eyes in an effort to destroy him and his family. No doubt man thought it was a good day's work. What he couldn't know was that by making the old fox blind he had enabled him to see, in his mind's eye, farther than any other fox, so that his wisdom had become a source of strength to all who sought his advice. How the old fox's own spirit had been strengthened when Skulking Dog had rescued her from the howling dogs; what a joy it had been for each of them to find that the other was still alive.

This, however, was no time to be thinking

back. There would be time for that as her cubs grew stronger. She would tell them all about Old Sage Brush; teach them all he had taught her: how to follow the Great Running Fox in the Sky and how to hunt by gloomglow. Outside her earth the light was now beginning to fade and soon the moon, which foxes call the wide eye of gloomglow, would appear in the sky. It would fill the earth with its comforting light and she would curl around her precious cubs and keep them warm while Skulking Dog went out to hunt.

Skulking Dog was a good hunter, a good provider. During the early part of the night he caught an unsuspecting pheasant which he took back across the frosty fields and gave to Sinnéad. However, he still had to eat himself, so he went farther up the side of the valley towards the evergreens. He was happy, and if the truth were known, very proud of himself for having fathered such a fine litter of cubs. He could just imagine how he would teach the little dog all the tricks, and the little vixens too, of course. He would tell them how he had outwitted the howling dogs to rescue their mother, and maybe even show them how to catch a hen. Sinnéad wouldn't approve of that but he would show them anyway At least the little dog fox would have to know what it was like to raid a farmyard. Times had changed but they couldn't forget all the old ways, otherwise life wouldn't be worth living.

The moon bathed the evergreens in its gentle glow and gave them a quiet majesty that man or creatures of the day rarely ever have the privilege of seeing. Skulking Dog was aware of their commanding presence as they stood silently silhouetted against the night sky, and he had a great urge to climb to the top of them and tell the whole valley his good news. He knew he couldn't, of course, but his high spirits took him up a larch tree that had been uprooted in a storm and blown against the other trees. How he expected to get down he didn't know, and was wondering how he could turn when a sudden sound solved his problem. It was the hissing and screaming of fighting animals, and so startled was he that as he looked up he fell off and landed with a thump. The pine needles broke his fall and he picked himself up, winded but otherwise unhurt.

The sounds were clearer now. They were coming from the direction of the black-thorns, and knowing that was where Hop-along had his earth, he sped off to investigate. Squeezing under the thorns, he was even more startled to see Hop-along locked in combat with four cats. They seemed to be all over him, biting and clawing, and clinging to him like seeds of goosegrass. Without hesitation he launched himself into the

46

attack, bowling both fox and cats over as he dived upon them, momentarily scattering the cats in all directions. The cats, however, weren't to be put off so easily and the next moment Skulking Dog found two of them around his own ears, while the other two resumed their attack on Hop-along.

Experience had taught Skulking Dog that when outnumbered the best thing was to go for the biggest and toughest opponent. He went for the large tom cat that was leading the attack. He found it fast, very fast, and it seemed for a while that he was snapping at shadows as it circled, sprang, clouted, retreated and attacked in a dizzy display of speed and ferocity. At the same time the cats must also have felt that they too were chasing shadows, for suddenly they turned, streaked in under the blackthorns, and disappeared.

FOUR

Moons of Death

Skulking Dog was about to take off in pursuit of the cats when Hop-along stopped him.

'It's no use,' he panted. 'They've gone back up to the evergreens. You'll never find them.'

'Are you hurt?' Skulking Dog asked him.

'I'm all right. Just a few scratches.'

'And what about She-la? Is she all right?'

Hop-along nodded. 'She's in the earth. I've blocked the back way in with thorns so they had to come round to the front.'

'But I've never seen cats act that way before.'

'They've gone wild, and I suppose they must have sensed our weakness. But they won't drive me out, not as long as I've a leg to stand on.'

Skulking Dog winced at the thought of that, knowing how handicapped and weak Hop-along was. 'Do you think they'll come back?'

Hop-along sank to the grass and licked his leg where one of the cats had torn it. Then he replied, 'Maybe, maybe not. But if they do, I'll be waiting for them.'

'So will I,' said Skulking Dog. 'If it's a fight they want, I'm the one to give it to them.' There was silence for a moment. 'How's hunting?' he asked.

'Hard enough,' conceded Hop-along. 'The cats have everything scared.'

'All right, you go back in to She-la. I'll hunt around and see what I can find. And don't worry. I'll be nearby if you need me.'

So saying, Skulking Dog loped off across the hillside. Even as he went, he felt the stinging pain of a dozen bites and scratches, but he had thought it better not to mention them to Hop-along in case the knowledge that the cats had found their mark might weaken his resolve. Anyway, he thought, they were only minor injuries and some day the cats would pay for them.

In a field beyond the beeches he spotted a rabbit feeding by the light of the moon. It was obvious that the presence of the cats in the area had made it very nervous, as it kept looking and listening for any more signs of trouble from the direction of the evergreens. When the danger came, however, it was from the other direction, and when it noticed Skulking Dog bearing down, it was too late. Skulking Dog took the rabbit back up to the blackthorns and gave it to Hop-along. Then he lay down in the frosty grass

49

and waited. If the cats came back he would be ready for them.

Back across the hill, at the other row of beeches, Sinnéad lay and watched as the soft rays of gloomglow flooded the entrance to her earth. Her four cubs were in another world, rocked to sleep by the rise and fall of her body. She had eaten part of the pheasant Skulking Dog had brought her and buried the rest for later.

It was the sort of night Sinnéad herself would like to have been out hunting. Bright and frosty. But it would be a long time yet before she would be strong enough and the cubs old enough to be left on their own. She wondered where Old Sage Brush was now and if she would ever see him again. Perhaps he would call when the word got around that she had given birth to four cubs. Perhaps Skulking Dog would meet him when he was out hunting and bring him back with him. Old Sage Brush, she knew, would be so proud of her. It was for the cubs they would have that he had taken the trouble of showing them some of the secrets of survival. The fur trappers had killed so many foxes, there were few of them, left. Now the future lay with their cubs. What was it the old fox had said? 'Now you are few but soon you will be many.' She wondered about She-la and how many cubs she would have. Vickey, she had heard, had given birth to two, and now she herself had four.

Something awakened Sinnéad from her reverie. It wasn't a sound. Nor was it a movement, or was it? Perhaps it was something she smelt or somehow sensed. She sat up with a start. Skulking Dog? Or was it Old Sage Brush? Then she saw them. Two small circles, each gleaming like the eye of gloom-glow, only green, then two more, and she knew by the smell now that it wasn't Skulking Dog or the old fox. It was cat! The hackles rose on the back of her neck, and she bared her fangs in an instinctive act of aggression, but the green moons stayed, only to be joined by two more, then two more.

Suddenly Sinnéad was seized with panic. She hoped Skulking Dog might appear and drive them away, although in her heart she realised that was only wishful thinking. She was alone and she must act. The agony of what she knew she must do gripped her heart and squeezed it until it hurt. She knew she must run and take one cub with her. But which one? In a few panic-filled seconds it was as if her whole life passed before her. She knew how proud Skulking Dog was of the little dog fox, but she was also aware of their terrible need to have more vixens so that they could have more cubs. Yet the dog fox was stronger and it was a fact of nature that the strongest always survived. The glowing green eyes were coming closer. The smell of cat was overpowering. What would she do?

In the end, Sinnéad acted on impulse. She grabbed the little vixen with the white spot on its forehead, the one that had been born in her own image, and bolted out the back of the earth. Blindly she tore through the brambles and thorns and kept running until she came to a secluded spot on the hillside where she had been in the habit of lying up during the day. There she dropped the cub and made a desperate dash back to the earth. Throwing caution to the wind she dived inside, determined now to take on those who had invaded her home. But they were gone, and so were her cubs. Frantically she charged out the other side and ran searching, sniffing the night air. However, the cats had taken separate ways and melted into the shadows, leaving a confusion of smells that were impossible to follow.

Not knowing what to do, Sinnéad now realised that she had left the other cub on its own, and fearing that the cats might have come across it, she bounded back up the hillside. To her great relief she found it lying where she had left it, mewling and con-fused, but safe. Curling herself around it, she lowered her head and sobbed quietly into her brush.

The moon had faded into the cold blue sky before Sinnéad's tormented mind lost some of its numbness. When the horror of what had happened to her cubs came flooding back into her consciousness, she gave vent to her agony with a scream that came from the very depths of her being.

Skulking Dog, who was still keeping guard outside Hop-along's earth, heard her, and realised at once that something was terribly wrong. He immediately sprang to life and raced to her aid. Vickey, who was lying up at the side of the quarry, also heard her, and knowing that the cry carried the sound of death, hurried across the hillside to see what was wrong. Black Tip, on the other hand, had hidden himself in the secluded field down at the bend on the river in the hope that the cock pheasants would come out again to fight. The water was rushing over the stones close by and he heard nothing else. Thus he was unaware of the drama that was taking place up on the side of the valley ... or of the one that was about to unfold.

Finding his sister and himself alone for the first time, Little Black Tip ventured towards the large gap of light that was the entrance to their den. Nothing stopped him, no friendly muzzle, no firm or reprimanding paw. He rocked back unsteadily on his hind legs for a moment, then pressed forward, fell over the small ledge of rock, and rolled down the pebbled path until he came to a stop in the grass beneath the brambles. Little Running Fox followed. She skidded down on all fours, crashed into him and went head over heels across him. Squirming back on to her feet, she called on her mother, but Vickey wasn't there to hear her complaint, so she followed her brother through the grass.

A few tufts farther on, Little Black Tip came face to face with what seemed to be another eye. It was a small white flower of wood sorrel, and after eyeing it for a moment he sniffed it, found it tickled, and sneezed. Regaining his composure, he led on, staggering across the floor of the quarry and up the far side. The path out of the quarry, they found, was steep, and twice they tripped on the loose stones and slid rather ungracefully back to the bottom. However, Little Black Tip was determined, and his sister wasn't far behind.

How long it took the cubs to get out of the quarry, no one will ever know. It's doubtful if they even realised they were out. All they knew was that they were in a jungle of grass that shed dewdrops on them as they passed, soaking them to the skin so that in no time at all they looked like drowned rats.

Their progress down the field, however, was neither fast nor furtive as that of a rat. Their manner was, to say the least, ungainly as they stumbled unsteadily along, flopping down here and there to rest and to wipe the dewdrops from their eyes. Where they thought they were going, not even they themselves could have had the slightest idea. And so they made their way along in this uncertain fashion of the innocent abroad, until they found themselves beneath the large chestnut tree at the foot of the long row of beeches. There they sheltered from a breeze that felt cold against their wet skin. They sat together and shivered until the nearness of their little bodies generated enough warmth to give them the strength and the spirit to continue.

Rising to his feet, Little Black Tip stared at a brown sticky bud on the end of a low sweeping branch. A small fly which had landed on it flexed its wings in a desperate but futile attempt to escape. Startled, the cub backed off, almost sitting on top of his sister. The fly flapped its wings again. Cautiously, Little Black Tip ventured forward, opened his large mouth and clamped it on the struggling fly. Immediately he pulled back, smacking and licking his lips as he swallowed the fly and at the same time tried to rid himself of the sticky substance that had held it.

Thus Little Black Tip scored his first success as a hunter! It was something that would have made his father very proud and no doubt would have been interpreted as a sign that he too would one day be a great hunter. It would also, of course, have caused much amusement and have made his mother wonder if he had intended swallowing the fly, or if his real intention had been to take the bud in his mouth in the mistaken belief that it was one of her teats! In any event, Little Black Tip seemed happy enough with his performance. Still licking his lips, he climbed up a ditch, closely followed by Running Fox, and slid down the far side into the meadow.

Fortunately, neither the crows nor the magpies noticed the two bedraggled creatures that pawed their way across the thick carpet of withered meadow grass. Perhaps they were too busy making plans for families of their own. Or perhaps it was just that the great god Vulpes had taken the two wanderers into his protective care and was smiling upon them in the same way that the wide eye of gloom-glow had smiled down on many generations of foxes as they set off on their nightly travels. Whatever it was, the two continued unnoticed and at long last reached the bottom of the meadow where, utterly exhausted, they curled up together and went fast asleep.

High above the rocky slope on the far side of the lake, the peregrine falcon circled ever higher in the currents of air. The valley was slowly coming to life and, like everything else, he was on the lookout for food. Even from that height, the black pupils of his dark brown eyes missed very little. He noted the meadow pipits and the reed buntings near the lake, but felt like something more substantial. Perhaps a wood pigeon, he thought. And so, with only a slight movement of his slate blue wings, he soared farther up the valley.

Unaware that such a thing as danger existed in their world the two fox cubs stirred into semi-consciousness and groped around for the familiar feel of their mother's teats. Not finding them, they awoke and tried to focus their eyes on something familiar. All they could see was each other, and all they could hear was their own snuffling and gurgling as they nosed around seeking to fill their mouths and their stomachs. However, there was nothing to be found and, feeling bewildered and confused, they stumbled on across the meadow grass until they came to a large patch that was greener than the rest.

Had they been old enough, the cubs would have been told of the dangers they might expect to encounter when they left their den, but they weren't, and so they continued across the bright green grass, blissfully unaware that if they *had* been older, it would have opened up and swallowed them. Because of the uncertainty of their step, they weren't even aware of the sagging of the swamp. Nor did they understand the occasional oozing and plopping of the mud around the edge.

The noise only served to make them curious and encouraged them to complete their hazardous crossing in one go. Had they stopped half way across the likelihood was that they would have fallen through. However, they reached the far side safely and succeeded in pulling themselves up on to a ditch, only to fall down the far side into a drain. There they found they had no option but to venture across the reddish-brown mud, and after a while emerged up through a gully on to a higher meadow that opened out into a heathery bog.

By now it's doubtful if even Vickey would have recognised the two cubs, they were so wet and dirty. It's also doubtful if the tall bird that stood among the tussocks of grass knew what they were. What is certain is that they didn't know what they were looking at. Even if they had understood what Vickey had told them about the long-legged corncrakes, it's unlikely they would have thought this was one, for it seemed to have only one leg and no head, and it was very big. Wide-eyed, they moved towards it. Hearing them, the curlew whipped its long curved beak out from under its wing, dropped the other leg and sauntered off in a somewhat jerky fashion. Just why the curlew chose to walk and not fly was something the cubs were better off not knowing. High above them, the eagle eye of the peregrine falcon had spotted the sudden movement of the curlew and, circling around, saw the two rat-like creatures disappearing under the heather. He circled again and waited.

Below in the heather, Little Black Tip and Running Fox stumbled on. Suddenly a crowing sound brought them to a halt. Steadying themselves against each other, they peered under a tunnel of heather at a gathering of white-feathered legs. As they watched, a small spider fell on the little vixen's nose. Shaking her head, she blew to dislodge it. Immediately the grouse, which had been feeding on small leaves of ling, burst into flight and glided across the heather.

Up above, the peregrine falcon swept over with a speed that was as swift and as sinister as an approaching shark, locked his wings and streaked down towards the heather. Only in the last few seconds did the grouse realise he was bearing down on them, and then it was too late. As they flapped desperately to get away, there was an explosion of feathers. One fell to the ground dead, and while the others glided to safety, the falcon quickly landed to claim his prey.

From under the heather, the two cubs looked out at the scattering of reddish-brown feathers. In the middle of them they could see enormous yellow claws. Looking up the feather legs, they saw a powerful, finely barred breast, and above that two dark eyes staring from blazing yellow sockets. The hooked blue-grey beak had already ripped the head from the grouse and, not realising that he was face to face with death, Little Black Tip took a few faltering steps forward.

FIVE

Flight of the Innocent

Ignoring the bedraggled thing that now tottered towards him, the peregrine falcon plucked the breast feathers from the grouse and proceeded to pick slivers of flesh from underneath. Each time he raised his head he stared at the small intruder in a way that would have signalled to a more knowing creature that here was a bird that had complete command of the situation. A more knowing creature, of course, would have been more furtive; perhaps it was this that puzzled the falcon and caused him to hold back.

Below the heather, little Running Fox sat and watched as her brother sniffed at the small downy feathers. They tickled his nose and he sneezed, blowing them into the air. The falcon turned his head and looked at him again. The cub ventured closer and, as he did so, the falcon lifted his prey, flapped his slate-blue wings and moved a short distance away. Little Black Tip followed.

Keeping an eye on him the falcon continued to strip the flesh from the grouse.

Then, without warning he took off and landed on a nearby post. Little Black Tip looked around. The great bird had gone. He could hear his sister mewling in the heather behind him. He turned and staggered towards her. Without warning, the falcon spread his wings, swooped down from the post, sank his powerful talons into the cub's puny back, and carried him off.

On reaching his earth, Skulking Dog had immediately detected the smell of cat, and recognised it as the same scent that still clung to his own fur after the fight up at Hop-along's. The earth was empty and he realised in a mixture of anger and despair that while he had been helping to protect Hop-along's home, the cats had invaded his own. Dashing out, he found Sinnéad and her one remaining cub sheltering in the hollow farther along the hillside. His heart sank. Seeing her lying there, curled around the cub and whimpering softly to herself it all became clear to him. He felt he had neglected her at a time when she had needed him most, and he was overwhelmed by a sense of guilt.

'What way did they go?' he asked her gently.

'Every way,' she sobbed. 'They split up and I couldn't follow them.'

He tried to explain what had kept him,

adding, 'I'm sorry, it's all my fault.'

Sinnéad shook her head. 'No. You were doing what you had to. If you didn't hunt we'd starve.'

'But if I'd come back instead of staying with Hop-along, I'd have been here when you needed me.'

'Hop-along and She-la needed you and you had no way of knowing the cats were going to come here.'

'I should have guessed that when we drove them off they'd go hunting somewhere else. I should have guessed.'

'You can't know everything,' whispered Sinnéad. 'And anyway, I should have stood my ground and fought them off.'

'How could you?' consoled Skulking Dog. 'There were too many of them. They'd have come in the back and trapped you, and then you'd all have been killed. Anyway, you weren't strong enough to fight them.'

'Still, I could have tried. I just panicked I suppose. It was the smell. It frightened me, so I just grabbed one and ran.'

'You did the only thing you could do.'

Sinnéad sobbed again. 'I'm sorry Skulking Dog.'

'You've no need to be sorry. You did well to save one of them.'

'I'm sorry I couldn't save the little dog for you. I know you'd have liked that.'

'You did what any vixen would have done.

You were faced with an impossible choice, and you did what you felt was right.'

'But was I right?'

Skulking Dog nuzzled her with his nose. 'Of course you were. We need vixens more than we need dogs. Remember poor Fang? He couldn't even get a mate. And anyway, how could you have left such a bright little star to die?'

Sinnéad tried to smile. She knew this was Skulking Dog's way of telling her that he understood, and it helped to hear him say it. But she still felt the pain of losing the others, and so she continued to cry softly to herself.

Vickey arrived a few minutes later, having hurried over as fast as she could. She flopped down beside Sinnéad, breathless and alarmed, and she too cried when she learned what had happened.

'Do you really think I did the right thing?' asked Sinnéad.

Vickey nodded. 'Of course you did.'

'Would you have made the same choice?'

'I don't know,' Vickey confessed. 'I really don't know. It's a choice I hope I never have to make. But Skulking Dog's right. You did what you thought was best, and that's what matters.'

'Vickey,' said Skulking Dog, 'will you stay with Sinnéad for just a little while. I must go to the evergreens.'

'I understand,' Vickey replied. 'I'll talk to

her until you come back.'

'I won't be long. But I must go. You know what I mean?'

Vickey nodded and Skulking Dog turned and made his way back up the side of the valley.

This was one visit to the evergreens, and probably the only one, that Skulking Dog would never remember. His mind was too numbed with grief, too overwhelmed by the enormity of what had happened. He would not recall going straight to the plantation instead of circling around to it as he would normally do. Nor would he remember searching the vast expanse of pine for traces of the cats that had killed his cubs. He picked up their scent all right, a scent he would never forget, but it was there a thousand times, everywhere and nowhere, and he searched and searched, criss-crossing the pine needles until he knew not where the scent started or where it ended. Finally, not knowing where to turn, he lay down and grieved quietly within himself. He listened to the wind in the trees, and he felt a loneliness he had never felt before, and he vowed he would avenge the death of his cubs. At the same time he knew he wouldn't do it alone, so he returned to his earth to take solace from Sinnéad and the little bright star that she nursed in her bosom. Seeing them comfort each other, Vickey slipped away to return to her own den in the quarry at Beech Paw.

Vickey was deeply troubled by what had happened and she tried to assess the implications of it as she made her way back. Once or maybe twice before she had come across cats that had gone wild, but not at cubbing time. This was something new and it held dangers for all of them. Judging from the experience of Hop-along and Skulking Dog, these cats had no fear of foxes. Now that they had successfully raided one earth, no earth would be safe. Vixens and cubs would need all the protection the dog foxes could give them, but if the dogs couldn't go out to hunt they would starve. Thinking of her own cubs now, she quickened her step and at the edge of the quarry gave an anxious glance back up towards the blackthorns. There was no sign of danger, so she hopped down into the quarry and picked her way across to the den. To her dismay, she found it empty.

Vickey's first thought was that the cats had come in her absence. Even as she sniffed around for some clue to what had happened, she was already blaming herself for going off and leaving the cubs on their own. Then she realised there was no scent of cat in the quarry. Whatever had happened, the cubs hadn't been taken by the invaders of Sinnéad's earth. Somewhat relieved, and finding the strength that comes at times of crisis, she bounded back up to the rim of the quarry. The dew was still on the grass and she could see the trail the cubs had left as they had made their way down the hillside. Realising the many dangers they could face, she raced after them. In a few moments she was at the foot of the chestnut tree and a pool of scent told her they had rested there. She also picked up Little Black Tip's scent on a low chestnut bud, but couldn't imagine what he had been doing. Anyway, it didn't matter. The question was where were they now?

Vickey followed their scent across the ditch, but lost it in the meadow. For some reason the withered grass hadn't held the dew either, and there was no trail to be seen. Undecided, she looked down towards the lake on her left and wondered if they had taken the fox path under the fallen ash. There was nothing to indicate that they had and, on instinct, she rushed straight down the meadow towards the bog.

This was a route no adult fox would take because the swamp at the bottom would bar their way. However, she could now see that the swamp had not stopped the cubs. They had left a clear trail across the bright green grass. As the danger of what they had done penetrated her distraught mind, she pranced this way and that to try and see which was the shortest way around, and hurried after them.

Picking up their scent again at the edge of the heather, Vickey also got a whiff of curlew, and a little farther on, the strong smell of grouse. Where had they got to? she wondered. How would she ever find them under the heather? What if they wandered into a bog hole? That would be the end of them. They would just disappear. Now she got the smell of blood. Game, she thought, but what was the predator? Man or beast? And what about the cubs?

Even as these scents and smells sent a variety of new thoughts and fresh fears through Vickey's mind, she saw the peregrine falcon swooping from the post and rising up a moment later with Little Black Tip clutched in his talons, and for the second time that morning the agonising scream of a vixen rent the air. If the great bird had swooped to pluck out Vickey's own heart, it couldn't have caused her greater terror and, as she watched her little dog cub being carried away over the lake, she now faced much the same choice that Sinnéad had faced when confronted by the cats. Should she follow the great bird in the hope of retrieving Little Black Tip, or should she search around for his sister Running Fox?

Fortunately, this was a decision Vickey didn't have to make. Black Tip, who was waiting at the bend on the river for the two cock pheasants to appear, heard her scream. At the same time he saw the great bird climbing overhead with Little Black Tip squirming in its talons. He too cried out and followed. Realising now that her scream had alerted Black Tip, Vickey quickly located the spot where the falcon had killed the grouse and in a moment she was beside the little mewling mess that was her vixen cub.

In normal circumstances, Little Black Tip would have been killed the instant the razor-sharp talons struck him, but because the falcon had just swooped from the post to pick him up, he was still very much alive. In fact, he was wriggling and squirming to try and get away from the thorns of pain that gripped his body.

Carrying a struggling cub back to his perch was also something new for the falcon and before he had climbed very far he decided to release his victim. Suddenly Little Black Tip found himself falling, falling, falling, and a moment later he dropped into the lake.

Seeing the splash, Black Tip bounded into the river. He was immediately caught in the current and swept down into the lake. Desperately he pawed the water and looked around for his cub. Then he saw him popping up to the surface, choking and spluttering before going under again. Frantically he tried to swim towards him, but found it impossible to get out of the current and knew that in a few moments he would be swept past the drowning cub.

To make matters worse, Black Tip now spotted a whiskered snout swimming towards the spot where the cub had gone down. 'No,' he barked. 'No!' However, his cry fell on deaf ears, for what he had seen was an otter and, as it dived towards the cub, its ears closed and it heard nothing. Instinctively, Black Tip also dived but, try as he would, he still couldn't break out of the current that held him like invisible claws.

In those few desperate moments, Black Tip feared that he would never see his dog cub alive again. Then, as he surfaced, he saw to his surprise that the cub had also come back up, and underneath he recognised the snout of his old friend Whiskers. 'No, Whiskers,' he cried, 'he's mine.' Before the otter could reply, he and the cub were also caught up in the current and all three were swept down the lake.

Now Black Tip himself was struggling to stay afloat, but as the otter came abreast of him, he could see that the cub was safe.

'Don't worry,' smiled Whiskers, 'I won't harm him.' So saying he turned on his back and held Little Black Tip in his webbed forepaws in the same way that an otter will hold a stone in moments of play. 'Now relax' he added, 'and let the current do the rest.'

Black Tip stopped struggling, paddling gently instead, and the two of them allowed themselves to be carried into the river where it left the lake. However, ahead of them now lay the farm. Already they could hear the sounds of dogs and man's machines. Realising the danger this held for them, they manoeuvred themselves towards the bank.

A short distance farther on, they came to a spot where the bank had been flattened by cattle drinking. Whiskers rolled over and dropped his precious cargo on to the mud. Finding a foothold, Black Tip climbed out after him, shook the water from his coat, and immediately started licking the life back into the cold wet rat-like body of his cub.

After a few moments the cub opened his eyes and began to splutter and cough. He was the most miserable looking little creature Black Tip had ever seen, but he was alive and that was all that mattered.

'I was afraid you were going to kill him,' he confessed.

'I guessed he was yours,' said Whiskers. 'Don't forget, the water is the otter's hunting ground and we're not likely to miss a fox either falling in or jumping in.'

'So you saw me going in after him?'

Whiskers nodded. 'But how did the great bird get him? How come you let him stray from your den?'

'I don't know,' Black Tip admitted. 'I was

71

hunting up at the bend on the river. Vickey was looking after them. I don't know what happened. It's not like her to leave them alone.'

He lifted the cub and carried him up on the meadow. 'But how do you come to be in the lake? I thought your hunting ground was back at the pheasant farm.'

Whiskers snorted to expel a few drops of water from his nostrils and said, 'So it is. But some nights I get the urge to follow the river.'

'For food?' asked Black Tip.

'Otters, like foxes,' smiled Whiskers, 'need more than food to survive. No, I think I might find myself a mate before I return. There are holts on the island in the middle of the lake.'

Somewhere beyond the farm the machines burst into life again, and Black Tip said, 'We'd better go. I think man must be building another bridge.'

Whiskers looked at him. 'You mean you don't know?'

'Know what?' asked Black Tip.

'Well, I haven't seen it myself, mind you,' Whiskers told him, 'but, according to the otters who live here, it's not a bridge he's building. It's a dam.'

SIX

Finding Fault

On the Mountain of Vulpes the billy-goat chewed his cud and looked out over the valley. His horns curved back from his dark forehead in a great arc so that they almost touched the white of his back. Together with the small beard on his chin, they seemed to testify to the fact that he had lived a long time on the mountain and perhaps had seen it all before. Indeed, he had seen many dramas played out in the valley, dramas involving sheep and foxes, hooded crows and ravens, and of course, man. But never before had he seen such a one as had been played out with the falcon that had come to make his home on the mountain. Now as he watched him return to perch on the rock face below, he realised that a new and powerful hunter had come to the Land of Sinna.

On the far side of the valley, Hop-along rested under the blackthorns. Somewhere nearby, wood pigeons were cooing in an old ivy-covered hawthorn. The ivy was their friend, giving them berries when no other food was available, and providing them with a nesting site that none could see and few could reach. Where, he wondered, would the thrushes nest? Wherever it would be it wouldn't be on the skimpy branches of the spindle trees, however much they liked to sport about in them. The spindle trees were now sprouting new shoots which were as straight and green as rushes, and like everything else they would soon be in leaf. There would come a day when the wind would turn cold and strip the hedgerow bare again, but not the spindle trees. He knew their seeds would turn to crimson to brighten the scrub and act like a beacon for the younger foxes when hunters forced them to run to earth.

When that time came, thought Hop-along, his cubs would be almost fully grown and beginning to make their own way in the world. That was, if he was going to have any cubs. He thought She-la would have given birth to them by now, but they were still waiting. In the meantime, she was growing moodier by the day, wandering off down to the meadows on her own, oblivious to any danger there might be.

High in the beeches to Hop-along's right, the rooks were swarming around their nests like bees, cawing harshly in what seemed to be a continuous swirl of confusion, while far down the valley to his left he could hear the sound of man's machines again.

Away below him he could see Black Tip returning to the quarry. He had something in his mouth and Hop-along assumed he had been out hunting. It was something he must do himself. He had been reluctant to go far from the earth in case the cats might return. However, there had been no sign of them since Skulking Dog had helped him drive them away. Anyway She-la was now down in the meadows, so he thought he might as well join her. On the way he would drop in and say hello to Black Tip and Vickey.

Vickey had brought Little Running Fox back to her den, and now as Black Tip arrived she dashed out to meet him. Seeing him carrying Little Black Tip by the scruff of the neck, and hearing the cub's plaintive cries, she took him and quickly put him back in the den too. She was overjoyed.

'I thought I'd never see him again,' she told Black Tip. 'How did you manage to get him out of the lake?'

'I'd never have got him, if it hadn't been for Whiskers.'

'Whiskers? I didn't know he was here.'

'Nor I. But he is, lucky for us. He spotted what was going on and kept the cub afloat. To tell the truth, I got a terrible fright. I didn't know him at first, and I thought it was another otter out hunting.'

Vickey, who had licked the cubs clean, now curled around them and let them suck the strength of warm milk from her body. 'They'll be all right,' she assured him.

Just then, Hop-along hobbled down into the quarry and lay beside Black Tip at the mouth of the den. Seeing the cubs so wet, he asked, 'What happened?'

Black Tip told him, and Hop-along added, 'Good old Whiskers. Well, I suppose he owes us a favour, after the way we helped him at the pheasant farm.'

Black Tip nodded. Somehow, he thought, the incident at the pheasant farm seemed so far away. It had happened during their travels with Old Sage Brush. Arriving at the river where Whiskers lived, they had found that a greedy mink was raiding a pheasant farm beside it and that the otters and foxes and everything else were being blamed. So together they had devised a plan to trap it, a plan that involved letting the water out of a small dam. The dam, he thought. How was he going to tell Vickey about the dam that was being built at the lower end of the valley? He was still wondering about that when he was aware of Hop-along talking again.

'The cats came to the blackthorns last night you know.'

'I know,' said Vickey.

'How do you know?' asked Hop-along.

'Skulking Dog told me he helped you fight

76

them off.'

'How many?' asked Black Tip, getting to his feet.

'Four,' Hop-along told him. 'But we drove them off. They went back up into the evergreens.'

'Not the evergreens,' Vickey told him.

'Where then?'

Vickey sniffed and swallowed hard. 'While Skulking Dog was up with you and She-la, the cats followed his scent back to his own earth.'

'Sinnéad?' said Hop-along.

Vickey's voice dropped. 'Sinnéad's safe. But they got three of her cubs. All she could save was one.'

'Oh no!' said Black Tip. 'Not the cubs!'

Hop-along got up, hobbled a few steps and lay down with his back to the den. His eyes had misted over and he didn't want Vickey to see.

Black Tip followed. 'It was my fault,' he said. 'I knew about the cats, and I was going to tell them. If only I'd done it sooner.'

'No,' said Hop-along, 'it was my fault. If Skulking Dog hadn't stayed on to help me, it would never have happened.'

'It was nobody's fault,' Vickey told them. 'We were all trying to help each other and things just went wrong that's all. I went to help Sinnéad when I heard her scream, and I nearly lost my own cubs. That doesn't mean she was at fault.'

'Perhaps we're all at fault,' said Black Tip. 'We've gone to great lengths to learn the secret of survival, and we've already forgotten the lessons we learned.'

'Black Tip's right,' said Vickey. 'And anyway, it's only cats that cry over spilt milk.'

'What can we do?' asked Hop-along. 'We're in the middle of our cubbing time.'

'We can do what Old Sage Brush taught us to do,' replied Vickey. 'We can use the cunning that the great god Vulpes gave us.'

'What do you suggest?' asked Black Tip.

'First of all I suggest you invite Sinnéad to come and stay here in the quarry. There's plenty of room for us all. Then you and Skulking Dog can take turns, one hunting, the other watching. Between the two of you, you can also keep an eye on Hop-along and She-la.'

Black Tip said nothing and, sensing that he had something on his mind, Vickey said, 'Is there something else? Something you haven't told me?'

Black Tip nodded. 'You remember what Ratwiddle said? About the water? Well, he must have known something we didn't know.'

Vickey shook off her suckling cubs and came out of the den. 'The lake? Is it rising?'

'No, it's not rising, said Black Tip. 'But it will.'

Alarmed now too, Hop-along got to his feet and asked, 'How do you know?'

'Whiskers told me. He says man's building a dam.'

'Where?' asked Vickey.

'At the far end of the valley,' Black Tip told her. 'Beyond the farm. Listen, can't you hear the machines.'

Vickey turned and went wearily back into the den. 'So that's what man has been doing all this time,' she said as she settled down again and allowed her cubs to resume their feeding.

Black Tip nodded.

'How long have we got?' she asked quietly. 'Long enough to rear our cubs?'

'I don't know. I doubt it.'

'What can we do?' she asked.

'We can run,' suggested Black Tip.

'Not me,' said Hop-along. 'And not She-la.'

'Nor me,' said Vickey and, turning to Black Tip, she told him, 'I know you mean well, but even if we could run, where could we go? A new territory would mean new dangers. No, at cubbing time there's only one thing we can do, and that's run to earth.'

'But if we stay, we'll be trapped between the cats and the rising water,' he pointed out.

'And if one doesn't get us, the other will,' added Hop-along.

Vickey sighed and was thoughtful for a

79

moment. Then she said, 'Let's not jump our fences before we come to them. This is the Land of Sinna, don't forget. Our land. This is the valley where Old Sage Brush said we would survive.'

'But how?' asked Hop-along.

'Remember what the old fox told us?' said Vickey. 'We must have faith in ourselves.'

'What do you think we should do then?' Black Tip asked her. 'We were his strength, but you were his inspiration.'

'I've already told you,' she said. 'Bring Skulking Dog and Sinnéad here, so that we can work from a position of strength.'

'But what can we do?' asked Black Tip.

'Man is still busy,' Vickey replied, 'so the dam can wait. But the cats are quiet. We must deal with them first.'

It never ceased to amaze Black Tip how a vixen could worry about something and then quite suddenly accept it. It was the same with having cubs, he thought. A vixen would get moody and irritable, and then for no reason at all her mood would change and she would be busy getting her den ready. They were strange creatures all right. Far more complex than dog foxes. But at least Vickey had accepted their predicament, and that was half the battle.

Leaving the quarry, Black Tip and Hop-along spotted a man with a walking stick trudging through the heather. He was a familiar figure, and one they were always careful to avoid. However, they could see by his manner that his eyes were on the ground in front of him, not on them, so they hurried about their business which was obviously more urgent than his.

Unknown to the foxes, the man on the bog had his own worries. He had made a modest living trapping foxes and selling their fur and had helped the local gun club to stock the heather with red grouse. Now he was going to lose his piece of bogland to the new reservoir for what he regarded as insufficient compensation. In the meantime, the demand for fox fur had ceased, and the foxes were free to prey on his grouse.

Coming to an open space in the heather, he turned over the remains of a grouse with the end of his blackthorn stick. Then he looked up the side of the mountain and scratched the stubble on his chin. Only the day before he had spotted a big dog fox with a black tip on his tail walking through the heather with a mouthful of wool. He had warned the sheep farmer many times about the danger of foxes. But the farmer had some queer notion about foxes. His little girl even had a pet one and walked it around like a dog on a leash. 'Mark my words,' he had told them. 'It'll turn on you. You can't tame a fox. It'll bite the hand that feeds it.'

Somehow he resented the sheep farmer. He envied his good grazing land and his big house, even the way he could control his dogs on the mountain. It wasn't right that some people should do better than others. But when the dam was finished the water would cover all their land equally, he thought. There would be no favouritism then. Looking back down at the mass of feathers at his feet, he stirred them again with his stick and vowed he would get the big dog fox that had killed it.

How right the foxes were. Here was a man who could see no farther than his feet. The peregrine falcon was away above his head. All he could think of was a fox.

Gathering up the remains of the grouse, the trapper returned to his cottage. There he lifted the latch of an outhouse door and went inside. Hanging from the walls were dozens of snares which had wrung the life from many a fox when the fashion for long-haired fur had created a demand for them and pushed up prices to a level they had never reached before. Under the snares hung dozens of steel traps which had caught countless rabbits when they were in demand. That was a time when many people had preferred rabbit to chicken, but the disease, myxomatosis, had wiped out the taste for rabbit, if not the rabbit itself, and deprived him of another source of income.

Ever since then most of the traps had hung in the shed, for when the fox fur had come into fashion he had used the snares as they had caused less damage to the foxes. He knew of one fox, for example, that had chewed off its leg to escape from a trap, and he had been afraid that a three-legged fox might not have been worth as much as one with four. Recently he had set a few of the traps to catch rats which seemed to have become more numerous. This was a phenomenon he blamed on the fact that his dog had died. It never occurred to him that it might be the result of there being fewer foxes to catch them.

Casting an expert eye along the rows of rusting traps, he lifted a handful of snares and selected two traps from underneath. Then, replacing the snares, he took the traps by the ring at the end of the chain and carried them out into the yard. To the un-trained eye, both looked the same, but he knew that with constant use some of them became weak. He remembered his youth when he used to wrap the teeth of weak traps in cloth and set them in streams to catch snipe for the big house. However, those days were gone. Now he had no use for a weak trap. He wanted a good strong one, one that would hold the big dog fox he had seen in the heather.

Setting the two traps down on the yard, he

pressed on each with his wellington boot and eased the jaws open. He knew from the tension which was the stronger. Then he returned the weaker one to the wall of the shed, stuffed a length of light rope into the pocket of his baggy jacket, and secured the door again. Taking the other trap, he made his way up through the fields towards the long row of beeches. Beyond the beeches, in the belt of blackthorn, he knew there was an earth and guessed it was occupied.

SEVEN

Cat and Mouse

There was a flurry of movement in a drain, and Ratwiddle bolted stiff-necked across the field and disappeared down through a hedge.

'Fool fox,' muttered the trapper. 'One of these days he'll catch that neck in one of my snares.'

Once more the trapper had misread the situation. He didn't know that poor Ratwiddle's neck had already been in one of his snares.

Climbing up the hillside towards the blackthorns, the man reflected on the fact that this was the second fox he had seen in the valley in the past few days. 'Stop shooting and snaring them,' he said to himself, 'and next thing you know they're all over the place.'

Hop-along was lying outside the blackthorns waiting for She-la to return from the meadows, when he became aware of the trapper crashing through a gap in a hawthorn hedge. He immediately turned and disappeared into his earth, pushed the blackthorn branch up out of the rear exit and made his way along the back of the blackthorns as fast as his three legs could carry him. He must warn the others, for if the man saw them carrying Sinnéad's cub into the quarry, they would all be in danger. And what if She-la was spotted returning from the meadows? He must hurry and warn her too.

The trapper looked in under the black-thorns. He could see the brown earth and he cursed the fact that his dog was dead. There was no way he could get in to set a snare. That's why he had brought one of the rabbit traps. The foxes, he grudgingly admitted, had picked a good spot, a warm sunny bank with their backs to the east wind and well protected. But he'd get them, one way or the other.

Beneath the blackthorns, the man's wellington boots, wet and shiny in the morning dew, touched a small bunch of primroses in the moss, two flowers and a bud. The bud was close-leaved like a rose about to unfurl, a resemblance that had given it the name, *prima rosa*, the first rose of the year. However, he wasn't looking for flowers.

Walking along the blackthorns, he came to a spot where they had thinned and given way to a patch of scrub ash and elder. Pushing the thorns aside with his stick, he squeezed inside.

Two thrushes took to the air in a flash of buff-coloured bodies. He saw what he was looking for, a spindle tree sprawling up through the bushes. Pegwood, he called it, but he did not know why. A more inquiring mind might have known that in days gone by this ungainly little tree, though barely able to support itself was highly prized for the hardness and toughness of its wood. It was used for many things, such as spindles in the spinning of wool, pegs and skewers. Country children had even used its straight shoots as knitting needles. Thus it had as many names as it had uses. The trapper, however, had a new use for it, for he knew well what its qualities were. He also knew that in its green state all he had to do was reach up with his blackthorn stick and the sturdiest branch would come away in his hand.

Beside a low stone wall that a farmer had once built to keep cattle out of the scrub, the trapper left his blackthorn stick and branch of pegwood on the grass. Next he emptied his pockets, leaving the trap, the grouse and the length of light rope down beside them. Taking two large flat stones, he set them on edge against the wall, about two feet apart, laid a third across the top, and placed the grouse inside. With a pen-knife, he now scooped a shallow, cross-shaped depression in the ground outside and put the trap into it. Then, starting at the trap, he cut a narrow trench in the grass, right around to where a large stone lay at the foot of the wall. Having done that, he tied the rope to the end ring of the chain of the trap, laid the chain and rope along the trench and tied the other end of the rope to the branch of pegwood.

Wiping his nose on his sleeve, he stood back to admire his handiwork and get his breath. Only a bit more and he would be finished. Bending down, he lifted the large stone and placed it firmly on the branch of pegwood. Then he got down on his hands and knees and packed small sods of grass on top of the rope and chain to cover them. Having pressed these down firmly with his feet, he walked back to the trap, flicked back the small brass tongue and stood on the lever. Having spread open the jaws, he laid the brass tongue across one side of them and hooked it under the central plate. He eased up his foot, the brass tongue held, the trap was set. All it needed was the pressure of a soft paw – any paw – on the central plate. The brass tongue would be released and the steel jaws would snap shut.

Finally, the trapper took the remaining grouse feathers and scattered them gently over the trap. Standing back he smiled to himself and nodded. He knew that if a fox missed the trap on the way in, it would almost certainly step on it on the way out, and would be securely anchored to the branch of pegwood under the stone. Picking up his blackthorn stick, he tidied up the grass and set off down the hill. He knew it might take two weeks for his scent to wear off, but he was in no hurry. The pelt would be no good to him anyway.

Hop-along had met Sinnéad coming across the side of the valley. She was carrying her cub, and was being escorted by Skulking Dog and Black Tip. They were taking no chances in case the cats might strike again. He warned them that the trapper was on the hill and, as they took cover, he hurried on down to the meadows in search of She-la. He knew she had gone hunting for frogs, a habit she had got into as her pregnancy advanced, and he hoped he would catch her before she headed back up to the black-thorns. Anxiously he sniffed around, lifting his head now and then to scan the most likely places. He picked up the fresh scent of Ratwiddle and knew by the pattern of his pawmarks that he had been in a hurry. At the same time, he realised that even if Ratwiddle had seen her, it would be a waste of time asking him where.

Pressing on, he at last picked up She-la's scent in a drain. He saw where she had been poking around among the watercress for frogs and, as he followed her scent on across the meadows, he realised to his dismay that she was on the way back. She had taken the fox path under the fallen ash and would surely run into the trapper. He thought of barking a warning to her, but knew that would alert the trapper too, so he hurried on, hoping against hope that he might catch up on her.

Hop-along, of course, wasn't to know that the trapper was carrying a blackthorn stick, not a gun, but he knew the man's presence meant trouble. Squeezing in under the hedge at the base of the chestnut tree, he hobbled up along the dry ditch beneath the long row of beech trees. Cautiously he emerged from the far end and stopped. Farther up the hill towards the blackthorns, two movements caught his eye. She-la was going up the hill as the man was coming down. He held his breath and waited. He saw both enter a hedge only a short distance apart. Then, miraculously, both emerged on opposite sides to continue on, oblivious to the presence of one another.

Heaving a huge sigh of relief, Hop-along hurried on, using what cover the hedges would provide. Somewhere nearby he heard the man climbing over a fence as he made his way back down the valley, and a few moments later he spotted She-la. She was sniffing around a low stone wall a short distance from the earth. In one awful moment, he realised that with the departure of the man, the danger hadn't passed but had been left behind at the blackthorns!

She-la was sniffing the grouse feathers when she heard Hop-along's warning bark. She lifted her head and looked towards him. Then, thinking he was warning her that the grouse was his, she turned and went into the blackthorns. Hop-along arrived at the wall a few moments later. In normal circumstances, he knew that the smell of the man would have alerted She-la to the danger, but with her cubs overdue her behaviour was anything but normal. He looked at the stones that encased the remains of the grouse. The moss was on the inside of the stones instead of the outside, and he knew they had been moved. He looked at the feathers sprinkled on the grass and he saw them for what they were, for he had seen the trapper's work before, and then it had cost him his leg.

Down in the valley, the trapper heard Hop-along's bark and smiled to himself. He was right, he thought. There were foxes up there.

When Sinnéad eventually arrived at the quarry, she chose a cleft in the rock at the foot of a tall arching dog rose, and said she would make her den there.

Knowing that, unlike brambles, the great

hooked thorns of the dog rose grow all the way down the stem, Skulking Dog said, 'But the thorns, they'll make it very difficult for you to get in and out.'

'If they make it difficult for me,' said Sinnéad, 'they'll make it difficult for them.'

Already, the others could see, the loss of her cubs had hardened Sinnéad in a way that encounters with man had not. They knew how man had blinded her father with the probing sticks and captured her, and how she had escaped only to be captured again. They had been there when Skulking Dog had rescued her, and they had heard her vow never to be taken by man again. But to lose most of her litter, that was even worse than falling into the hands of man. That was to lose something more precious than life itself. Now she was sheltering under the dog rose, and they knew how she felt. If the cats came again, the thorns would hurt them more than they could hurt her, for she was past hurting. Skulking Dog and Black Tip, however, were determined that she should be left in peace. It was time to strike back.

In the depths of the evergreens, the red squirrel sat on a high branch and nibbled a pine cone. His long bushy tail curled up over his back so that the fine hairs on its tip looked like a cockade above his head. While all his attention seemed to be on the cone, his alert eye was watching every movement below him. He himself had no need to hunt for food, but he knew that the creatures beneath him had.

Forests are one of the last refuges, not only of the red squirrel, but of the wild cat and, though there are no wild cats in Ireland, some instinct had no doubt made the evergreens the home of these cats that had gone wild. Where they had made their den, the squirrel didn't know. He was too busy looking after his own home. When the cats weren't foraging in the fields beyond, they were climbing the trees in search of nests. That meant his own nest was in danger, and so he spent much of his day playing hide-and-seek with the cats, drawing them away from his young and returning only when it was safe to do so.

The cats, he knew, had been out of the forest during the night, and now they had surrounded a larch tree containing a magpie's nest. They were well aware that the squirrel was watching them. They had come to accept his presence and the fact that they couldn't catch him. However, they weren't aware that two foxes were also watching them, for while cats may have good sight, their power of scent is not as highly developed as is that of the fox.

Black Tip and Skulking Dog took stock of

their enemies. Ratwiddle hadn't been far wrong when he had said that all cats looked black in the dark. These ones even looked black in the shade. Their leader was a large long–haired tom–cat with a black back, black legs and black-tipped tail. Yet his face had the grey and black stripes of a tabby cat and, coming down from his eyes, these gave him the ferocious look of a tiger. His body was as big as that of a young fox, thought Black Tip, but his legs were shorter. The she cat was similarly marked, but was smaller and thinner, like the two younger cats. Even so, they all had a tough rangy look about them, a look which showed that they didn't depend on man for their food.

Now as the foxes watched, the younger cats climbed the larch tree. Two magpies swooped in to defend their nest, protesting noisily with each flick of their long black tails. With a less obvious, but more sinister flick of their tails, the two older cats sat back and waited.

'Let's take them,' whispered Skulking Dog. 'The older ones first.'

Black Tip, however, cautioned otherwise. 'Their legs are shorter, but they can climb trees. We must get them out in the open where they can't run away.'

Realising the wisdom of what Black Tip was saying, Skulking Dog readily agreed. He knew it was the sort of wisdom Old Sage

Brush had taught them to use, so they also sat back and waited.

The young cats soon found that the magpies could tease and torment just as well as they could. Bit by bit they found themselves being drawn out along branches that were too thin and brittle to support their weight. In the end, they must have decided there were easier ways to get food. As if at a given signal, both beat a hasty retreat down the tree and jumped to the ground, whereupon all four ran off through the evergreens towards the blackthorns. Up above, the squirrel streaked through the trees ahead of them, while the two foxes followed at a discreet distance.

Emerging from the evergreens, the black pupils of the cats' eyes narrowed until they were mere slits in pools of green. Everything was quiet so they cautiously tip-toed their way down the side of the valley.

Suddenly they sensed that they weren't alone and turning, found themselves looking up at the amber eyes of Black Tip and Skulking Dog.

The foxes sprang, and once again the quietness of the blackthorns was broken by the hissing and screeching of creatures locked in combat. Even in the depth of his earth Hop-along could hear it and hurried out to investigate. Seeing what was happening, he immediately hobbled up the hill to

95

help. With the arrival of a third fox, however, the cats broke off the fight, and short and all as their legs might be, reached the evergreens before Black Tip or Skulking Dog could stop them.

'Sorry about that,' said Hop-along as they sat down and watched the cats in the trees above them.

'You were only trying to help,' said Skulking Dog.

'This is going to be a long wait,' Black Tip told him. 'You better go back and look after She-la.'

Hop-along nodded. He realised that this was a situation where four legs might cope, but courage on its own couldn't.

As the day wore on, the cats became restless. From their vantage points on four different trees, they had sat staring at the two foxes lying on the ground. Then, as if by clockwork, they sprang into action, streaking down one tree and up another, clouting and clawing the foxes as they passed. So fast were they that neither Black Tip nor Skulking Dog knew which way to turn. Nor did they know when or where the next attack was coming from. If they charged after one, another would be on their tail. If they turned to snap, a passing claw would clip their ear.

Eventually, during a brief respite, Black Tip whispered, 'You know, we're not winning this fight.'

'Maybe not,' replied Skulking Dog. 'But we can still wait it out.'

Black Tip nodded. 'We can, but our vixens can't. There'd be no victory in letting them starve.'

In his heart Skulking Dog knew his friend was right, and so they withdrew a short distance and waited. Seizing their chance, the cats descended from the trees and disappeared.

High above, the red squirrel followed them, but the two foxes turned and made their way back to Beech Paw.

EIGHT

Springing the Trap

When Black Tip and Skulking Dog had left the quarry Vickey had talked to Sinnéad until she and her surviving cub had drifted off to sleep. Then she had curled around her own cubs again and thought of all that had happened.

It seemed that, almost in a twinkling of an eye, their dreams had been shattered. How much Old Sage Brush had shown them, she thought, and how little they seemed to have learned. How could all these things be happening in the valley where, according to him, the fox would survive? Somehow it didn't make sense.

Like the other vixens, she had been looking forward to a time of peace and quiet, a time when she could rear her cubs in safety and teach them all the things they needed to know, but no sooner had cubbing time come, than things had started to go wrong. First the cats had come to prey on them, then the great bird from the mountain. If that wasn't bad enough, man had returned to set his traps. But worst of all was the discovery that

98

their valley was going to be flooded.

Vickey was thinking that perhaps the time had come when they should send for help, and was about to say so to Sinnéad, who had just wakened, when Black Tip and Skulking Dog returned. She could see they were bleeding from many small cuts and scratches, and asked them, 'What happened?'

Between them, they told her, and Black Tip added, 'Their leader is a big tom-cat, as big as the one that attacked you. We just couldn't get them down out of the trees.'

'And we couldn't stay all day,' explained Skulking Dog. 'We have to hunt.'

'That settles it then,' said Vickey firmly. 'We need help.'

'But where will we get it?' asked Black Tip. 'What other fox would be free to come?'

'Old Sage Brush would,' said Vickey. 'And Fang. He didn't mate, remember?'

'But Sage Brush is very old,' Skulking Dog reminded her. 'He can't help us fight, any more than he can help us turn back the water.'

'He helped us once before,' Vickey reminded him, 'when we thought all was lost. Maybe he can help us again. Don't forget what he told us about this valley.'

'But that was just foxlore,' said Skulking Dog.

'Maybe so,' insisted Vickey, 'but he said it was this valley that the great god Vulpes had chosen so that we could survive. Perhaps he knows something about it that we don't.'

'Well I suppose it's worth a try,' said Black Tip. 'And even if Fang came it would be a great help.'

Sinnéad slipped out between the thorns of the dog rose, and Skulking Dog asked her, 'What do you think Sinnéad? Do you think we should send for Old Sage Brush?'

Sinnéad lay down beside him, and nodded.

'All right,' said Skulking Dog. 'Let's do it.'

While Skulking Dog stayed behind to watch over the vixens and their cubs, Black Tip set off to let the old fox know that they needed his help once more. However, this time it was a double invitation that he left wherever he put his mark; and when he barked the name of Old Sage Brush into the wind, he also let the foxworld know that he wanted his good friend Fang to come too.

Suddenly it was like old times. First the old fox had come, then Fang. Old Sage Brush was delighted to be reunited with his daughter Sinnéad again, but deeply saddened to learn that she had lost three of her cubs. Fang hadn't mated after leaving them, and was as strong and independent as ever. Bit by bit they told them what had happened.

With his fur in moult, Old Sage Brush seemed to have become greyer and more frail since they had last seen him and, as they talked, he lay curled up with his white whiskers resting on the end of his tail and listened. When they had finished he lifted his head and, looking with unseeing eyes at the sky, said, 'The cats are not like many of the other animals we know. They're hunters, like we are. They are not loyal to man, like the dog. Like us they will not be put on a leash. And it is because they are so like us that we find them such able adversaries.'

'If they are like us,' said Black Tip, 'how can we beat them?'

'They are like us in some ways replied the old fox, 'and in that respect we can understand them. But they are not like us in other ways, and that is where we can defeat them.'

The others knew from experience that the old fox was telling them there was a way to beat the cats, but that they must sit down and work it out for themselves.

'We could draw them on to the snapping jaws,' suggested Skulking Dog, referring to the steel trap that had been set by the trapper.

However, the old fox rebuked him, saying, 'I know how you must feel, but that is man's way, not ours. Anyway, there are four of them and it takes only one leg to close the snapping jaws.'

'We thought we could get the better of them because they have shorter legs than we have,' said Black Tip.

'That was good thinking,' the old fox told him, 'but they also have other shortcomings, and you must find those too.'

Knowing how well Old Sage Brush knew and liked the valley, and was able to find his way around in it in spite of his blindness, Vickey was reluctant to tell him about the dam. However, when she tried to break it to him gently, she was surprised to learn that he already knew about it.

'But you said this was where the fox would survive,' Vickey reminded him.

'And so it will,' replied the old fox.

'How can we survive if man floods the valley?' asked Black Tip.

'The water may rise,' the old fox assured them, 'but your earth will stay dry.'

'I don't understand,' said Skulking Dog. 'You know these things, yet you cannot see. We can see, yet we did not even know man was building the dam.'

'There are many things you do not know,' the old fox told him. 'But you must believe what the great god Vulpes has told us, and you must believe in yourselves.'

'What about the great bird that hunts the skies above the Mountain of Vulpes?' asked Vickey. 'Should we try and drive him out too?'

Old Sage Brush shook his head. 'He is no threat to you. The skies are his hunting ground, not yours. The mountain is his home, and mine.'

'Can we find you there if we need you again?' asked Black Tip.

The old fox shook his head. 'You must stay away from the mountain. There is great danger there for those who do not know its ways.'

'But what if we need you again?' asked Vickey.

'You will have no further need for me,' he told her. 'You know all you need to know.' So saying, he nuzzled his daughter Sinnéad and the little she-cub, and made his way out of the quarry.

The other foxes were confused by many of the things Old Sage Brush had told them, just as they had been confused by many of the things he had said to them in the past. However, they knew their first priority was to get rid of the cats, and now that they had Fang to help them guard their cubs, the dogs could hunt, and they could all try to figure out what to do.

The setting sun had inflamed the sky beyond the mountain of Vulpes, and from the branches of the fallen ash a blackbird sang its last and most beautiful song of the day. Down among the lengthening shadows, Black Tip searched for Ratwiddle. Two magpies were flitting in and out of their nest in the sturdy willow at the edge of the lake.

For once they were quiet. That meant Ratwiddle must be hunting elsewhere, so Black Tip slipped quietly past. It had occurred to him that Ratwiddle seemed to know more about some of the things that troubled them than anyone else, apart from Old Sage Brush. Mad as he might be, it was he who had foretold that the water would rise. It was also he who had spoken of black cats in the dark. If he could have visions like that, perhaps he could be far-sighted enough to tell them what they could do to get themselves out of their predicament.

Black Tip made his way along the lake shore to the clump of reeds they called fox tails. The light was fading fast now and the wind from the mountain had turned chilly. As always when he looked at the mountain, he couldn't help thinking of the old fox's story of how the great god Vulpes had caused the wind to blow and created the valley as a place where the fox could survive. He wondered what it meant, and somehow he couldn't help feeling that it was very far removed from the problems they now faced. Not for a moment did he doubt the old fox's wisdom. The problem was to understand it.

Ratwiddle was lying in the reeds scratching himself. As usual, a dead rat lay beside him.

'Do you never tire of rats?' asked Black Tip.

Ratwiddle stopped scratching and studied the question for a moment before answering slowly, 'No. It's them or me you see. The water's rising and they're dragging me down.'

'Is there no way to stop it?' asked Black Tip.

Ratwiddle twisted his head up around and scratched himself again. 'No. It's rising and no one can stop it. I see it every time I close my eyes. It's always the same. It's the rats you see. They're dragging me down.'

'And what about the cats?' asked Back Tip gently. 'Do you see any cats?'

'The cats are like fleas,' said Ratwiddle. 'They make you scratch your head.'

Black Tip looked at him, unsure as always if he was talking nonsense or saying something profound. 'How can we get rid of them?' he asked.

'Cats are like fleas,' Ratwiddle repeated. 'They won't go away, no matter how much you scratch.' He himself, however, seemed to get a sudden urge to go and, without another word, picked up the rat and ran stiff-necked into the gloom.

Not knowing what to make of him, Black Tip headed off up the valley to hunt. For the first time since he had learned of the cats, he felt more at ease. Ratwiddle hadn't been much help to him but with Fang keeping one eye on the cubs and the other on Hopalong he knew they had got themselves a breathing space. Fang, he felt, would be a great source of strength to them. He might have lost his fight for Vickey, but he probably still had a soft spot for her and would stick around long enough to see them through the difficulties that lay ahead. As for Old Sage Brush, he hadn't stayed long, but then he had his own life to lead and, being blind, his need for protection was probably the greatest of all. No doubt he felt more at home over on the mountain.

Black Tip was turning these things over in his mind when it suddenly occurred to him what Ratwiddle had said. That was it, he thought. Why didn't he think of it before? Ratwiddle had told him how to get rid of the cats, and he had not had the sense to realise it!

'But what did he say exactly?' asked Vickey when Black Tip told her.

'He said that cats are like fleas. They won't go away no matter how much you scratch them.'

'We don't need Ratwiddle to tell us that,' said Skulking Dog. 'We are the ones who end up with the scratches.'

'But don't you see,' insisted Black Tip. 'We must get rid of them the same way we get rid of the fleas, by driving them into the water.'

Sinnéad, who had been listening behind the dog rose, came out and joined them. 'You're right,' she said. 'That's one of their shortcomings. They don't like water.'

'But how do we pull the wool over their eyes?' wondered Skulking Dog.

'There must be a way,' said Black Tip. 'Maybe Fang and Hop-along can think of something.'

Taking care to avoid the snapping of jaws at the low stone wall, Black Tip made his way along the blackthorns. He found Fang lying near the entrance to the earth and, hearing the sound of their voices, Hop-along joined them.

'What we need,' said Black Tip, 'is some way to get them out of the evergreens and keep them out.'

'Bait,' said Fang. 'We need something to tempt them out far enough and long enough for us to get between them and the ever-greens.'

'You won't find better bait than me,' suggested Hop-along. 'I can use the snapping jaws. It's time we put them out of action anyway.'

The three of them talked well into the night, and when Black Tip reported back to Skulking Dog and the vixens, only one problem remained.

'How do you force them into the water once you get them there?' asked Sinnéad.

Vickey agreed. 'It'll be difficult to keep them from doubling back up to the ever-greens.'

'When Black Tip and I chased them into the evergreens,' said Skulking Dog, 'they took refuge in the trees. Maybe we could drive them towards the large willow.'

'What good will that do?' asked Vickey.

'Well,' explained Skulking Dog, 'if we can get them into the willow, perhaps the magpies can do the rest.'

'You've got it,' cried Black Tip. 'They may be able to climb trees, but they're no squirrels!'

She-la was asleep and the morning dew was still on the grass as Hop-along made his way along the blackthorns. Pausing to pick up a short piece of rotting branch, he approached the low stone wall. The smell of the trapper was still there, even stronger than the grouse. Cautiously he circled the spot where the man had sprinkled the feathers. From his previous experience he guessed that the snapping jaws were in the centre. Edging as close as he dared, he raised his head and tossed the branch over on to them. He was right. Immediately the toothed jaws of the steel trap clanged shut with such force that it jumped and spun over on to its back. Hop-along jumped too, but now he knew that the trap could no longer harm him. Lifting it by the chain, he pulled until the rope was uncovered. Then he wrapped the rope around his foreleg and began to yelp and scream and roll around in the grass.

From a hiding place near the evergreens, Black Tip and Skulking Dog watched and waited. What, they wondered, if their plan didn't work and the cats didn't come? A short time later, however, the arrival of the red squirrel told them that the cats were on their way. They held their heads low as their breath was misting slightly in the morning air, but they needn't have worried. The two younger cats arrived first, bounding out of the evergreens and down the hillside. The older cats followed, but with somewhat more caution. Stopping at the edge of the trees, they carefully took stock of the situation. For a moment it looked as if they were going to stay put. Then another agonising scream from Hop-along filled them with a curiosity they couldn't control, and they also raced down to the blackthorns to investigate.

Seeing the three-legged fox struggling with the trap, the cats now believed the way was clear to raid his den and hunt for rabbits over by the beech trees. First, however, they couldn't resist teasing him. Noting how far he could go before the rope brought him down, they gathered around and started to hiss at him and strike at him with their paws.

Had they been more watchful and cunning they would have known that Hop-along was now playing the cat and mouse game with them that he had played with the rabbits using the snare. And had they been more alert, they would have seen him drawing his foreleg clear of the rope. But they weren't and didn't realise they had been tricked until he charged. Taken by surprise, they scattered towards the blackthorns, only to be confronted by Black Tip and Skulking Dog who had slipped out underneath to cut them off. Without stopping, they swerved and raced down and across the side of the valley towards the beeches. There they found their way barred by Fang. Swerving again, they bounded back towards the quarry. Again they were blocked, this time by Vickey and Sinnéad. Black Tip and Skulking Dog were now hard on their heels, so they took the only course left open to them and fled down into the valley.

Knowing that it was important to keep them in full flight, Black Tip, Skulking Dog and Fang followed in hot pursuit, and didn't stop until they had chased them right up into the large willow tree at the edge of the lake. Then the three dog foxes sat down in a semi-circle and waited.

The magpies who nested there were furious and started up with a continuous chatter of protest from the top-most branches. In doing so, they only drew attention to their nest, with the result that the cats, in a way that is peculiar to their species, soon forgot about the foxes and started climbing towards the large ball of twigs in search of food.

Quietly the foxes sat back and watched as once again it became the turn of the cats to be teased. The cats, of course, thought they were getting closer and closer to the birds. They didn't realise that they were being drawn farther and farther away from the nest. Suddenly they found themselves out on a limb, and unlike the branches in the evergreens, these were willowy limbs that would neither sit still nor give them support.

Seizing his chance, Skulking Dog rushed forward with such speed that it took him right up into the tree, and began snapping madly at the clinging cats. One by one, the cats dropped into the water, only to be driven out into the lake by Black Tip and Fang.

It was clear to all that the cats didn't like the water, but it was also equally clear to the cats that there could be no turning back. They kept going until the current of the river caught them, and a short time later the foxes saw them pulling themselves up on to the muddy island in the middle of the lake, dripping wet, dejected and defeated.

Up at the quarry, Vickey and Sinnéad turned and went down to their cubs.

NINE

Needle Nine

The days were getting longer and slightly warmer. The chestnut buds had become big and shiny, and their scales had opened back like ladybirds' wings. The catkins on many of the willows had grown fat and fluffy like climbing caterpillars, and now edged the lake with a band of gold as bright as gorse. Another band of gold ran along the hillside as more primroses came into bloom before the blackthorn buds could cut off the light. Already the spindle trees had got their first slender leaves, and even in the shade of the quarry, the great arching stems of the dog rose were turning a leafy green.

The past few days had seen a big change in the cubs. They had become stronger and more active, although it would be a good while yet before they were weaned. They had also become more demanding, but occasionally the vixens would shake them off to go out and look across at the island. It was a great comfort to them to know that the cats were still there. But while that threat had been removed, they were ever aware that a much greater threat remained. Thus they were also looking down to assure themselves that the lake wasn't rising. Ratwiddle's dream had become their nightmare. The noise of the machines was a constant reminder that the threat now came from man.

'It's our own fault,' said Vickey. 'We forgot that man is our greatest enemy. We stayed away from him when we should have stayed close to see what he was doing.'

'I saw what he was doing,' admitted Skulking Dog, 'but I didn't know it was a dam he was building. I thought it was another bridge.'

'Well, we'll have to watch him from now on,' said Vickey.

'What do you want us to do?' asked Black Tip.

'I want you to go down the valley with Skulking Dog to man's place.'

'And then what?'

'Just watch and let us know what you see. Fang can stay here and keep an eye on the rest of us.'

'And, Skulking Dog,' said Sinnéad as they got up to go, 'I'm feeling hungry again. But be careful you don't draw any danger on to us. We've enough problems.'

Up in the blackthorns, Hop-along now found that he could go about his business without having to look over his shoulder at

113

the evergreens. It had been a great strain on him, not knowing when the cats would descend on She-la or himself, and it was with much satisfaction that he lay and watched them crawling around the island. The Island of Cats, he had decided to call it, and he felt it was good enough for them. They might find enough to eat on it, if they tried hard enough, and they would pose no threat to the otters whose young would be safely behind the water line.

At the same time Hop-along continued to feel ill at ease. The waiting time was always the worst, he thought. She-la had become more restless and her trips to the meadows more frequent. Not that she needed to hunt for herself. He and his friends had provided her with all the food she would normally want, things like rabbit and pheasant. However, she didn't seem to be interested. All she wanted was frogs. It was a longing that seemed to come over her at the oddest times. Even in the middle of the day he would see her getting up and trotting off down to the meadows.

'Imagine,' he told Fang, 'nothing but frogs.'

Fang smiled. 'Well, just between you and me, Black Tip told me he found Vickey nibbling pine cones when she was waiting for her cubs to come. She just couldn't resist them. Imagine eating pine cones when she had plenty of other food. All she had to do was dig it up.'

'It's funny all right,' agreed Hop-along.

'Have you told her about the dam yet?'

Hop-along shook his head. 'I can't. Not just now.'

'I know what you mean,' said Fang. 'Anyway, there's no reason why she should know now. You can tell her later.'

It was now the time of year man calls Easter. The gorse bloom was at its best and brightest, and Skulking Dog and Black Tip were aware of its strong distinctive scent as they made their way across the hillside. The valley contained plenty of woodland and patches of scrub, so there was no shortage of cover.

Skulking Dog was pleased that his mate had sufficiently recovered from the shock of losing her cubs to want to eat. The free-range hens that he had often watched down at the farm were now almost within smelling distance so the thought of an old-fashioned raid on an open hen run excited him. Black Tip, however, reminded him that Sinnéad had also asked him to be careful. She might be hungry but for the moment she was safe, and anyway, that wasn't what Vickey had sent them out to do.

Soon they were looking down on the cluster of farm houses that nestled around the lower end of the lake. As they watched, their attention was drawn to a single-decker bus that was wending its way down a twisting road on the far side of the valley. On a slow bend, a line of men armed with cudgels forced it to stop, and one of them, a man with flaming red hair, climbed aboard and looked at the passengers before allowing it to continue. It seemed that foxes weren't the only ones not welcome in the Land of Sinna.

At the cluster of houses, the bus stopped and a young boy got off. He was in denim jeans and carried a small suitcase. The bus drew away and for a moment the boy stood and looked around. Then three sheepdogs scurried out and ran around him, and close on their heels came a girl with long fair hair and wearing jeans. She shouted a greeting as she ran and hugged her visitor.

As the two young people walked arm-on-shoulder into the yard, Black Tip whispered, 'Look!'

'I see them,' said Skulking Dog.

'I don't mean *them*,' said Black Tip. 'Look, just inside the gate.'

'It's a fox!' exclaimed Skulking Dog, hardly able to believe his eyes.

Black Tip had spotted the fox watching from the side of one of the gate pillars. What was more, as the two young people and the dogs went towards the house, it ran after

116

them. Only the boy and the two foxes on the hill thought it strange. Neither the girl nor the sheep-dogs paid any attention to it.

'What an odd way for a fox to behave,' remarked Skulking Dog.

'What an odd way for man to behave,' said Black Tip.

'Old Sage Brush told us that man and fox once lived as friends in this valley,' said Skulking Dog, 'and it looks as if some of them still do. Come on, let's tell the others what we've seen.'

'You go,' said Black Tip. 'I'll wait until gloomglow and then try and have a word with this fox. Maybe it can tell us more than we'll find out by watching.'

'Good idea,' replied Skulking Dog, 'but be careful. I'll try and catch some food on the way back.'

As the day drew to a close, a fresh breeze began to blow in across the lake and black clouds appeared over the Mountain of Vulpes. Almost as if man was expecting the weather to change, Black Tip could see him rounding up the sheep and lambs and taking them into the shelter of the lambing sheds.

By the time darkness had spread across the valley, so had the clouds. There was no gloomglow and Black Tip was just as glad. With the clouds covering the moon, it would be darker in the farmyard, and safer.

When he judged the time was right, Black Tip raised his head and barked. Down at the farm the sheepdogs began barking, and he knew by the muffled sound of their bark that they had been locked in for the night. In the darkness, the vertical pupils of his eyes had opened wide, but it was his sense of smell that told him where the other fox was. Its unmistakable scent led him to a wire pen at the back of the barn.

'I thought you were a free fox,' he whispered through the wire.

'So I am,' came the reply. 'I stay here at night. This is my home and I've a warm bed in this box in the corner. But who are you?'

'I'm Black Tip. Who are you?'

'I'm Needle Nine.'

'But if you're free, why do you stay here, Needle Nine?'

'I like it here. Willow is good to me.'

'Willow?'

'She found me when the trapper killed my parents, and took care of me.'

'But don't you find danger here, so close to man?'

'There is much danger in this valley,' replied Needle Nine. 'But not for me. It's you who are in danger.'

'We know,' said Black Tip. 'That's why we want to talk to you.'

Just then the sheepdogs, sensing the presence of a strange fox, began barking again, and somewhere nearby a door opened, sending a shaft of yellow light across the yard.

'You must go now,' warned Needle Nine. 'I'll meet you again tomorrow night.'

'Where?'

'Down by the lake.'

'But how can you get out?'

'I'll find a way. Hurry.'

When Black Tip returned to the quarry, he found the others still talking with Skulking Dog, and now they crowded around him to hear what he had to say.

'You mean it's a prisoner?' asked Sinnéad when he told how he had found the other fox locked in a pen.

'Not in the way you were,' said Black Tip. 'It says man is its friend.'

'That's right,' said Skulking Dog. 'When we saw it at the gate there was no one holding it. It was free to come and go as it pleased.'

'But if it's free, why do they lock it in at night?' wondered Sinnéad.

'That's where it sleeps,' explained Black Tip.

'You mean it doesn't hunt at night?' asked Fang.

'It says it has no need to,' Black Tip told them. 'Man feeds it.'

'What name does it go by?' asked Vickey.

'Needle Nine. It's a dog fox.'

'And what age is this Needle Nine?' she asked.

'He's very young. Only about half grown. I'd say he was from an early litter. The trapper killed the rest of them.'

'Yet these people are good to him,' said Sinnéad. 'I wonder why?'

'And they're the ones with the sheep,' remarked Skulking Dog.

'Strange,' agreed Vickey. 'And what did he tell you?'

'I didn't have much time to talk to him,' said Black Tip. 'The dogs were barking. But he said we were in danger, not him.'

'So he must know about the dam,' said Vickey.

Black Tip nodded.

'Then I shall have to meet Needle Nine.'

'But is it safe for you to go?' asked Black Tip. 'You're still weak.'

'The storm will give us all the protection we need,' Vickey replied. 'Man doesn't like the wind and will go to earth, but in times of trouble we have always found it to be a good friend.'

Later that night, Vickey and Sinnéad went up to see She-la in the blackthorns. Until now they had been too busy with their own cubs to visit her. Vickey was worried about her, and she also thought that if Sinnéad were to worry about her too, it might help to take Sinnéad's mind off her own problems.

They met Hop-along just inside the earth, and Vickey inquired, 'How is she?'

'Okay. She's down below.

'No sign of any cubs yet?' asked Sinnéad.

Hop-along shook his head, and Vickey asked him, 'How many are you hoping for?'

'I don't mind,' he told her, 'as long as they're all right.' So saying, he thanked them for calling and hobbled off into a side chamber. He was leaving them to say to She-la whatever vixens usually said to each other on occasions such as this.

In fact, there was very little Vickey and Sinnéad could say to She-la, so they tried to cheer her up by joking about her fad for frogs.

'It was the pine cones that tormented me,' Vickey told her. 'Imagine, pine cones. I think it must have been the smell of them. Poor Black Tip, he must have thought I was turning into a squirrel!'

She-la nodded and smiled, but her smile couldn't conceal her unspoken concern for her own situation, and they found it difficult to talk to her. They couldn't tell her about the dam, and they certainly couldn't tell her what had happened to Sinnéad's cubs. And so, when she asked Sinnéad how many cubs she had, Sinnéad simply replied, 'Just one, a little vixen.'

'What are you going to call her?' asked She-la.

'Twinkle, said Sinnéad on the spur of the moment.

121

She-la looked at her. 'Why Twinkle?'

'Because,' Sinnéad told her, 'she carries my mark, and she's the only little bright star we have.'

Vickey didn't say anything, but she knew Sinnéad was telling She-la something she hadn't told Skulking Dog. However, she was sure Skulking Dog wouldn't mind, especially if it helped to cheer up She-la. Anyway, naming cubs was something that was better left to vixens.

TEN

Night of the Big Wind

The familiar figure of the billy-goat was missing from the mountain top, and the peregrine falcon was no longer in the sky. The bearded guardian of the Mountain of Vulpes had decided to seek a more secluded spot from which to watch the valley, and he knew that the sky hunter had folded his wings and was perching below him on the ravens' nest. The wind was whistling around the crags and rushing down the ravines to the lake. Every now and then it shattered the surface and sent great shadows across the water. Sometimes it seemed to the old goat that it was he who was in the sky, for even though he had moved farther down the clouds had followed him, and after a while he could see no more.

In all of the valley, there was now only one tiny pocket of calm where the wind couldn't reach, and that was the quarry at Beech Paw. Like the billy-goat and the falcon, the foxes listened to the wind whistling over their heads, and thought their own thoughts. They worried about the dam and when the lake would rise, and they wondered what they could do about it.

Oblivious to the wind, the cubs were fast asleep, and Vickey thought about the journey she and her friends had undertaken with Old Sage Brush. In particular, she recalled how they had lost their way after the clouds had obscured the Great Running Fox in the Sky and they could no longer follow it. All the vixens had been in cub then and the dog foxes had worked so hard to get them back to Beech Paw.

Now she wondered what they had come back for. The cubs with which they had hoped to swell their numbers had already been decimated. Sinnéad and herself were lucky to have three between them. She-la would be lucky if she had any at all. The future which, on their return, had looked so bright, seemed bleak. The threat of the dam hung over them as heavily as the clouds which now swept across the valley.

'Black Tip,' Vickey whispered, 'where would I find Ratwiddle?'

'Why, what do you want him for?'

'He was able to tell you how to get rid of the cats, wasn't he?'

'You're wasting your time,' said Black Tip. 'I asked him about the dam.'

'Still,' said Vickey, 'I'd like to talk to him.'

'Well, you'll probably find him down at the fox tails. He never strays far from there.'

Vickey thanked him and made her way up out of the quarry. Immediately the wind caught her fur and flicked it a thousand and one ways at a time. She raised her head and found that the wind brought many scents from near and far. She looked over at the beeches to watch the wind bending the mighty trees, now a mass of swelling purple buds. Behind her the blackthorns stood strong and unbending, supporting the spindle trees and providing cover for the small birds and other creatures that had sought sanctuary in their depths.

The wind had also brought back the cold, but Ratwiddle didn't seem to mind. Vickey found him lying as usual in the great reeds at the edge of the lake, his long neck raised stiffly in the wind among canes which were bending almost to breaking point.

'I thought I might find you here,' said Vickey.

Ratwiddle kept his eyes closed as if listening to the sound of the wind in the reeds.

'You were a great help to Black Tip,' she went on. 'We were able to drive the cats on to the island.'

Ratwiddle didn't answer for a moment, and she felt the wind was having a soothing effect on his poor tormented mind.

'That's where the rats should be,' he said at last. 'Then they wouldn't drag me down.'

'What can we do to stop man flooding the

valley?' asked Vickey. There was no reply, and she went on, 'But Ratwiddle, you wear man's collar. You must know him better than any of us. There must be something we can do to stop him.'

'No,' said Ratwiddle slowly. 'There is nothing we can do. The water's rising, rising...'

'But Ratwiddle,' pleaded Vickey.

Ratwiddle, however, made no reply, and Vickey knew that his mind was somewhere up there in the wind and that he was no longer with her. Disappointed, she returned to Beech Paw.

Throughout the day the wind continued to blow and, when darkness fell, Black Tip led Vickey and Fang up out of the quarry. Sinnéad had asked Skulking Dog to stay with her, and the others understood.

Shielding Vickey as much as he could against the driving wind, Black Tip found the night darker than ever he had found it before. In fact he couldn't see far beyond his nose, but he had a general idea of the path he should take, and instinct did the rest, instinct and Needle Nine, that is. The young fox located them down at the lower end of the lake and brought them up to the shelter of a thatched cottage that nestled in the side of the valley.

On a grassy knoll at the back of the

cottage, Needle Nine settled down and the others did likewise. It was obvious that the young fox had been there before. They were level with a back window and they could see down into the cottage. A turf fire was burning in the hearth. Sitting around it were an elderly couple and the boy and girl Black Tip had seen at the farm. The wind whistled across the thatch and, as it dropped for a moment, Needle Nine told them, 'I often wait here for Willow.'

'This danger you speak of,' said Vickey. 'Do you mean the dam?'

'So you know about it,' replied Needle Nine. 'Why then are you still here?'

'We've come to find out more about it,' said Fang.

'They're going to flood the valley,' Needle Nine told them, 'and we're all going to have to go.'

'We can't go,' said Vickey. 'It's our cubbing time.'

'When will it happen?' asked Black Tip.

'I don't really know,' said Needle Nine. 'But I don't think it can be long. The dam's nearly built.'

'How far will the water rise?' Vickey asked him.

'Who knows? But all the animals in the valley are in danger. You must leave before it's too late.'

'We've only recently returned from a long

127

journey,' said Black Tip. 'The Land of Sinna is our home.'

Inside the cottage, a similar conversation was taking place.

'But that's terrible,' said the boy. 'That means you'll have to leave.'

'How can we leave?' said the old man. 'Glensinna's our home. It's always been our home. My father and mother lived here before me, and their parents before them.'

His wife rocked in her chair on the other side of the hearth and nodded. 'The council's plans to turn Glensinna into a huge reservoir has cast a shadow over our lives for some time now.'

'But can you not stop them?' asked the boy.

'We've tried everything,' said Willow. 'We've even gone to court. Isn't that right, Grandad?'

The old man nodded. 'That stopped work on the dam for a while, but we lost, and it's only a matter of time now before they finish it.'

'Is there no other way to stop them?' asked the boy.

'There's some who say only violent action will stop it now,' said the old man. He took out his pipe and a plug of tobacco and, as he peeled the tobacco into the palm of his hand with a pen-knife, he added, 'I suppose it'll come to that in the end.'

'Is that why those men stopped the bus when I was coming here?'

The old man cupped his hand around the bowl of his pipe so that the tobacco slid into it, packed it with his forefinger and lit it. 'That would be it all right.' He puffed on his pipe. 'Had one of them foxy hair?'

The boy nodded.

'That would be them all right. They say there's only one way to stop this business.'

'Violence never solved anything,' said the old woman. She got up to put more turf on the fire, and it was obvious she was a bit agitated by the whole affair.

'This will be the biggest disaster to hit Glensinna since the Night of the Big Wind,' Willow told her cousin.

Outside the window, Needle Nine pricked up his ears. In spite of the wind, his sharp hearing could pick up the sound of Willow's voice. If only he and his friends could have understood what she was saying. But, of course, all the conversations that took place between the foxes were in their own language. Had they known man's talk, they would now have heard the old man tell his version of the story Old Sage Brush had told them.

'The Night of the Big Wind,' repeated the boy. 'What was that?'

'It was the night a great wind blew over

129

this country,' explained the old man. 'A wind the like of which has never been known before or since.'

'Oiche Na Gaoithe Mhór,' said the old woman in Irish. 'The Night of the Big Wind.'

'It was in 1839,' the old man told the boy. 'It started to rain before lunch-time. Then everything became very still and warm. By evening the wind had begun to rise. By ten o'clock a gale was sweeping across the country from the south-west, and by midnight hurricane-force winds were tearing everything apart. Trees all over the country were levelled. Even oak trees that had withstood the storms of 200 years were torn up by the roots. They say it was the worst night for centuries.'

The old woman poked the fire and the wind drew a shower of sparks up the open chimney. 'God forbid there'll ever be a night like it again,' she said, more to herself than anyone else.

'By early morning the winds were at their height,' the old man continued. 'Buildings were blown down, church spires and chimney stacks came crashing to the ground, and there were people killed.'

'How?' asked the boy.

'Oh, falling bricks and stones, that sort of thing. They say some poor unfortunates were even blown into the bogs. Others died when their homes went on fire.'

'How did that happen?' asked the boy.

The old man paused to re-light his pipe. The wind howled around the cottage, and the two young people pulled in closer to the fire.

'The thatch, I suppose,' the old man told him. 'It must have fallen in on the open fires. Cottages burned, from one end of the country to the other.' He puffed his pipe and gazing into the glowing sods of peat just as the others were now doing, added, 'It was a dreadful calamity. Town and country, rich and poor, they all suffered. The storm swept right across to parts of England, Scotland and Wales, and caused havoc there too. Who knows what damage it did at sea.'

'*Oiche Na Gaoithe Mhór,*' repeated the old woman quietly to herself.

'But how did it affect this valley?' asked the boy. 'Did the Big Wind cause some disaster here?'

'Indeed it did,' said the old man. 'It was several days before the gales died down. There was a lot of rain, and then the rain turned to snow. It must have affected the mountain. In the middle of the night, when everyone thought the Big Wind was over, there was a massive rumbling here in the valley, and when folk awoke next morning they found that there had been a huge landslide. Half of the mountain had slipped down into the valley, burying some of the cottages on the far side of the lake.'

'What a terrible thing to happen,' remarked the boy.

'It was after that, that the foxes started to warn us,' said Willow, who had sat quietly listening to her grandfather, having heard him tell the story many times before.

'The foxes?' said her cousin. 'How?'

'After the Night of the Big Wind,' explained Willow, 'whenever any danger threatened the valley, the foxes would move to the mountain, and people knew it was a sign that something was going to happen. Isn't that right, Grandad?'

The old man nodded. 'The last time it happened was when the forest caught fire. The foxes must have sensed something was wrong. The people saw them going and got out just in time.'

'They haven't moved yet,' said the old woman. 'So maybe that's a good sign.'

The old man sighed. He knew his wife still clung to the hope that even at this late stage the council would abandon its plan for the reservoir. He wasn't so hopeful.

'Because of what the foxes did for the valley,' Willow went on, 'they were never killed here. But when fox fur came into fashion, things changed. The trappers made a lot of money from the foxes and some people say it has brought nothing but bad luck.'

'It's true,' the old man agreed. 'It was only

when they started trapping them that things started to go wrong.'

'But Willow's good to them,' said the boy.

'Willow's very fond of foxes,' said the old man. 'Did you see her pet, Needle Nine?'

The boy nodded, and outside the window Needle Nine pricked up his ears again at the mention of his name.

'Why did you call him Needle Nine?'

Willow smiled. 'Because he was always doing damage around the house. His teeth are like needles, so I had to keep a close watch on him when he was smaller. You know, a stitch in time. That's why I called him Needle Nine.'

Continuing his story, the old man said, 'It was because the fox had become very special to the people here, almost like a warning light in times of trouble, that they called the valley Glensinna.'

'Not just Glensinna, Grandad,' Willow reminded him. 'Glensinna Bawn.'

'But what does it mean?' asked the boy.

'It's from the Irish explained the old woman. 'Gleann an tSionnaigh Bháin. It means the Valley of the White Fox.'

Outside the window, the cold wind swept down from the mountain and curled around the foxes. Vickey had been telling Needle Nine the story Old Sage Brush had told them. It was the story of how the fox god

Vulpes had caused a great wind to reshape the mountains and form the Land of Sinna, and how he had put a great white fox to rule over it and entrusted him with the secret of survival.

Slipping away from the grassy knoll, Needle Nine went back to the farmyard, and the others returned to the quarry at Beech Paw.

ELEVEN

Feeling like Fleas

During the night, lightning lit up the Mountain of Vulpes, peals of thunder rumbled over the valley, and it began to rain. The wind drove the rain across the lake in great sheets. Nothing ventured out. Down in the farms, man lay listening to the thunder and imagined great rocks crashing down the mountainside. Up at Beech Paw, the foxes curled around their young and listened to what they thought was the voice of Vulpes. In their mind's eye, both man and beast could see the windswept lake and the dam, and they wondered when the water would rise and force them to move.

The crow of a cock pheasant awoke Black Tip, so he bounded up to the rim of the quarry. The storm had blown itself out, the sky had cleared and the sun was up. The storm seemed to have stolen none of the lustre from the willows, but the reeds had taken on the tattered appearance of foxes in moult. Up in the evergreens, the wind had stripped the catkins from the hazels, but they had already withered and it was their

135

time to fall. Some of the larch trees that had taken the brunt of the storm had lost their grip and toppled against the spruce. Otherwise, there was little damage and the valley was almost back to normal.

Because of the storm, the foxes had been unable to hunt during the night and, as the dog foxes prepared to set out, Vickey looked across at the Mountain of Vulpes. The billygoat was back on his favourite spot above the rocky slope, and the falcon was circling overhead. But her mind was on the one she couldn't see, Old Sage Brush.

'We must talk to him,' she said. 'We must find out what to do.'

'Would you like me to go?' asked Black Tip.

'I'll go,' said Fang. 'You and Skulking Dog must hunt. Your vixens are hungry.'

'All right,' said Vickey. 'But be careful. The old fox told us that the mountain holds danger for those who do not know it, remember. I think we should take his advice and stay away from it. You could leave out messages for him the way Black Tip did. That should be enough.'

'I'll go with you as far as the river,' said Black Tip, and off they went together down the storm-washed fields.

The river was in flood after the night's heavy rain, and while Fang made his way up along it in search of a place to cross, Black Tip concealed himself in a hawthorn hedge at the secluded bend in the hope that the cock pheasants might come out to fight. If they didn't he would look around for hen pheasants or any other birds that might have been blown away from their usual haunts during the night. One way or another he knew they wouldn't go hungry.

The sun was rising now, and once again Black Tip could feel its warmth. Soon it would dry out the fields and the flowers, and the bees would be busy again. For the moment, however, the fields were his and his alone.

Thinking the same thing, a cock pheasant strode out across the grass. Black Tip had always been convinced that birds had a poor sense of smell, and now he was sure of it. Unaware of his presence, the pheasant crowed and watched the far hedge with furtive glances. A short time later another cock raced into the fields and when the two of them met they puffed out their golden-red neck feathers, lowered their beaks and stared at each other. Next moment they met in mid-air with a crash of wings and a flurry of clawing and pecking.

However, both survived the first round uninjured and crouched and stared at each other again. Black Tip had seen a cock fight before so he knew this ritual of staring and striking would go on for some time. He also knew that somewhere nearby was a smaller buff-coloured hen pheasant, otherwise the cocks wouldn't be fighting. Yet experience had taught him that things often came easier to the fox who was prepared to wait, and after about half an hour his patience was rewarded. Without warning, the two cocks parted and ran in different directions. It wasn't apparent which one was the victor, as no feathers had been pulled, or blood spilt. However, the one that ran towards Black Tip soon found that it was the loser.

Shortly after Black Tip and Fang had left the quarry, Needle Nine had arrived and, when Black Tip returned with the pheasant, he found Vickey and Sinnéad telling the visitor about their journey with Old Sage Brush.

The vixens had found that, because he was being reared by man, the young fox knew little or nothing about the ways of the wild, and he stared wide-eyed as they told him how they had been guided on their journey by the Great Running Fox in the Sky.

'But I have never seen this Great Running Fox you speak of,' said Needle Nine.

'You will only see it if you know where to look,' said Sinnéad.

Seeing the young fox was puzzled, Vickey smiled and told him, 'During our cubbing time, the Great Fox in the Sky knows we do not travel and therefore do not need its guidance, and so it waits around almost directly above us.'

Needle Nine looked up, but could see nothing.

'You can only see it at gloomglow,' said Sinnéad. 'It waits up there and watches over us until it is time for the young to strike out on their own.'

'When is that?' asked Needle Nine.

'When the nights start to grow longer,' said Vickey.

'Then you will see the Great Running Fox taking off across the sky beyond the hills,' said Sinnéad, 'and you will know it's time to go.'

'Does that mean we just follow it?' asked Needle Nine.

Vickey shook her head. 'No, for it too travels far. But each night mark its position well before you start, and you will know what way to go.'

Just then Ratwiddle arrived and dropped down beside them.

'We were just telling Needle Nine about the Great Running Fox in the Sky,' Vickey told him.

'The Great Running Fox has no head,' said Ratwiddle.

'But it has,' protested Sinnéad. 'It's there if you want to see it.'

'All I see is the water rising,' replied Ratwiddle. 'It's up around the fox tails.'

'Is that right?' Vickey asked Black Tip.

Black Tip shrugged. 'It may be up a little, but it's just after last night's rain. The river's in flood.'

'But the machines are quiet,' said Vickey. 'Man hasn't finished has he?'

Needle Nine shook his head and told her: 'There's still more work to be done.'

'Still, I don't like it,' said Vickey. 'I think the sooner we have a look at the dam the better.'

'You can probably see it from the evergreens if you look hard enough,' suggested Needle Nine.

'Good idea,' said Vickey, 'We'll go up as soon as Fang returns.'

The red squirrel sat in a larch tree at the edge of the evergreens nibbling a hazel nut he had stored last autumn. The cats had gone, but he was keeping an eye on the foxes who had gathered beneath the tree. He had often seen foxes in the evergreens before, of course, but not so many of them.

Apart from Sinnéad and Skulking Dog, who were minding the cubs at the quarry, and She-la who was in her earth, they were all there – Black Tip and Vickey, Fang, Hopalong, Needle Nine and even Ratwiddle.

'Can you see it?' asked Needle Nine.

'Do you mean that white thing?' asked Vickey.

Needle Nine nodded.

'And what are the yellow things around it?' asked Fang.

'They're the machines that make the noise,' Needle Nine told him.

'I think you'd better have a closer look at it,' Vickey said to Black Tip.

'Why?' asked Hop-along. 'What can we do about it?'

'Surely you haven't forgotten,' said Vickey. 'We've destroyed a dam before. Who knows, maybe we can do it again.'

Hop-along, who was also straining his eyes to try and see the dam, said, 'What do you think, Ratwiddle?'

Ratwiddle lay over on his side and began to scratch himself. The others moved discreetly back. 'The water has already reached our tails,' he said. 'The fleas have started to jump.'

At this, the others jumped back. Ignoring them, Ratwiddle scrambled to his feet and ran off through the plantation, head in the air as if keeping an eye on the squirrel who streaked through the tree-tops ahead of him.

On the way back to the quarry, Vickey called in to see She-la, and Hop-along settled himself at the entrance to the earth. Down below he could hear them talking as She-la worked away at the small chamber where she would have her cubs. She was

141

preoccupied with a concern to have it just right, and he thought to himself that the other vixens knew best. There was no point in talking to her now about things that might or might not happen. All she knew was that the most important thing in her life-cycle was going to happen, and at this time nothing else mattered. Anyway, he could do the worrying for her. What else did a dog fox have to do, except hunt for food, and watch and wait? Nevertheless, it was a big moment in his life too and, between thoughts of floods and dams, silly thoughts flitted through his mind. He found himself wondering if his cubs would be like him or She-la, and he hoped they would be like her as he wanted them to have four strong legs, not three like him.

Vickey interrupted his reverie, saying as she emerged from the earth, 'She-la's fine, you've nothing to worry about. She's just a little late, that's all.'

'How many do you think she'll have?' asked Hop-along.

'It's hard to say. She's big. It could be three or four.'

'As long as they're all right,' said Hop-along. 'That's the main thing.'

'Of course they'll be all right,' Vickey assured him, 'and I'm sure the dog foxes will be like you.'

Hop-along shook his head.

Suddenly it dawned on Vickey what Hop-along was worrying about, so she smiled and told him, 'Yes they will, especially if they're born with courage and cunning.' She thought for a moment. 'You must tell them about our journey with Old Sage Brush, and don't forget to tell them how you helped Whiskers the otter to trap the greedy mink at the pheasant farm. If it hadn't been for cunning like that we'd never have survived.'

Hop-along nodded but said nothing. He may have felt taller, but he knew he still had only three legs. Furthermore, he had a feeling that whatever his fears for the cubs, this dam that now threatened them wasn't going to be as easy to destroy as the one at the pheasant farm.

Nature demanded that the vixens should remain close to their earth. Their cubs needed constant attention, they themselves lacked the strength to travel, and even if they did feel up to it they wouldn't have the speed to escape from any danger they might encounter. And so, while Skulking Dog remained behind to guard the quarry, Black Tip and Fang made their way down the valley towards the farm where Needle Nine lived. The young fox had promised to link up with them again and take them as far as the dam.

By now the sun had soaked up the rain and they found that the scents had become good and strong again. The rooks were back feeding in the fields, apparently unruffled by their buffeting in the beeches, and there was a tempting flavour of rabbit in the hedge-rows. However, once again hunting would have to wait.

Needle Nine led them in a wide uphill sweep until they were well beyond the farm buildings. Below them they could see the river becoming gradually wider as it meandered through the valley. Using all available cover, the young fox took them along at a fast trot until they reached a small beech wood. There he stopped and peered over into the trees. The others sensed now that they hadn't far to go.

Overhead, a multitude of nesting rooks cawed and clung to the slow-budding branches. Beyond the wood they followed Needle Nine into a dry ditch covered with brambles. This ditch, they discovered, led to another, and then another, and they were glad the young fox had come to show them the way.

At last they emerged into the open. Needle Nine stopped and looked ahead. Black Tip and Fang pulled up beside him. Their mouths dropped open and they gasped at what they saw. They were at the narrowest part of the valley and there standing before them was the biggest dam they had ever seen. Their eyes followed the sloping mass of white concrete up to the sky, and their heats sank. It was so big it made them feel like fleas.

'It's not finished yet,' said Needle Nine.

Black Tip realised his mouth was open and pulled his jaw back into place. 'You mean there's more?'

'The middle part isn't built yet,' explained Needle Nine. 'That's the part that will stop the river.'

'And flood the valley,' said Fang almost absentmindedly. His eyes were still trying to take in the enormity of it all.

Black Tip looked at the giant yellow machines that lay idle in the fields. 'And they're the things that make the noise?'

Needle Nine nodded. 'Man uses them to build the dam. See what they've done to the fields.'

Now as the others looked around, they saw the huge brown scars the mechanical diggers, the bulldozers and the lorries had carved across the valley floor.

'They're very strong,' added Needle Nine. 'They can shift ditches and hedges, even trees if they get in their way.'

Black Tip sighed. 'How are we going to tell the vixens?'

Fang shook his head. 'If only they could see it for themselves. They'd know how hopeless it is.'

'Maybe it's best if they don't,' said Black Tip. 'Come on, let's go back.'

TWELVE

Talking to the Animals

Two peregrine falcons now circled the Mountain of Vulpes. A female had come inland to take up residence in the ravens' nest. The sky was cold and clear, and to the billy-goat it seemed that the clouds had dropped to the floor of the valley. Even the sharp eyes of the falcons couldn't penetrate the early morning mist, so the two birds soared farther up the valley in search of food.

Vickey lay on the rim of the quarry. For the first time in a long while she couldn't see the Island of Cats, but her mind was now on the mountain. 'I wonder why Old Sage Brush didn't come?' she wondered and, finding she was unable to think of an answer, she went down to where the other foxes were lying and asked them.

'I left the message for him anyway,' said Fang. 'Right over as far as the mountain.'

'He said we knew all we had to know,' Black Tip recalled.

'But do we?' asked Vickey. 'We don't know when the dam will be finished, or how far the water will rise.'

146

'The dam is big,' Black Tip told her. 'It's very, very big.'

'Bigger than anything we've ever seen before,' said Fang.

'How high?' asked Skulking Dog.

'As high as the sky,' replied Black Tip.

'Only the mountain is as high as the sky,' said Sinnéad.

'And a mountain it might as well be,' Fang told her.

'Even mountains can be moved if the great god Vulpes so wishes,' said Vickey.

'But you should see it,' said Black Tip. 'It's like a mountain of stone.'

'How much remains to be built?' asked Vickey.

'Only the part that will stop the river,' Fang informed her.

'If only Old Sage Brush was here to advise us,' said Vickey. 'I wonder why he didn't come?'

'He told us there was a way to get rid of the cats,' said Sinnéad.

'And he did say our earths would stay dry when we asked him about the dam,' Black Tip reminded them.

'But how could he know?' wondered Vickey. 'He can't even see the dam. Unless he was saying there is something we can do about it if we put our minds to it.'

Black Tip sighed. 'You wouldn't say that if you had seen it yourself.'

Hop-along had arrived now and lay down beside them.

'Remember,' said Vickey, 'when we returned from our journey, and I asked Old Sage Brush if we had learned enough to survive the attacks of man?'

'I remember,' said Sinnéad. 'He said that if the lowly beetle could overcome the mighty elm, could not the cunning of Vulpes overcome the work of man.'

'That's right,' said Black Tip. 'And I said there were many beetles, but few of us.'

'And he said,' Skulking Dog recalled, 'that soon we would be many.'

'But surely he was referring to your cubs,' said Fang.

'Maybe so,' said Vickey, 'but there are other foxes.'

'Not many,' Skulking Dog reminded her.

'But what can we do,' asked Black Tip, 'even with the help of other foxes? The dam is very tall, you can't imagine what it's like.'

'What is taller than the larch?' asked Vickey. 'And yet you saw it yourself up in the evergreens. Its roots are so shallow that even a summer storm can topple it.'

'What has that to do with the dam?' asked Hop-along.

'Well, we know the dam is tall, and we know it is long, said Vickey. 'But is it deep? If its roots are shallow like the larch, then perhaps all is not lost.'

148

'You mean we could try and weaken its base?' asked Sinnéad.

'By burrowing under it?' said Skulking Dog.

'Why not?' Vickey replied. 'Who knows what we can do until we try.'

As the others reflected on this possibility, Black Tip and Fang looked at each other. It was easy for Vickey to talk. She hadn't seen the dam. Then Hop-along asked, 'But who will do all this digging?'

'If enough foxes can't help us,' said Vickey, 'perhaps there are other animals who can.'

Skulking Dog sat up with a start. 'What other animals?'

'Badgers,' suggested Vickey.

'Badgers!' exclaimed Fang, remembering how he had once been booted out of a badger set.

'Yes, badgers,' repeated Vickey. 'Aren't they the best diggers you could wish for? Who, I ask you, can dig a better earth than a badger?'

They all knew the truth of that, for they had lived in badger sets more often than they had lived in an earth dug by themselves.

'Which other animals might help us?' asked Black Tip.

'Animals who can dig,' replied Vickey. 'Rabbits, even rats.'

Black Tip was now sure that his mate had taken leave of her sense. 'But we're their enemies,' he pointed out. 'Why should they help us?'

'Because by helping us they'd be helping themselves,' explained Vickey. 'If the valley is flooded, they will lose their homes too. And don't forget all the other animals. The stoat for example, and of course – the one that knows more about dams than any of us – the otter.'

'But Vickey,' argued Black Tip, 'you're talking about small animals like rabbits and rats. We're talking about a dam that's so big it makes even us look like fleas by comparison.'

'Maybe so,' insisted Vickey, 'but how big is the beetle compared with the elm? If they can do it, why can't we?'

'But Vickey,' went on Black Tip, 'there is no way we can destroy this dam.'

'I'm not saying we can,' said Vickey, 'but if we could even delay it, just long enough to get our cubs weaned, that would be enough, wouldn't it?'

The dog foxes could see there was no point in arguing, so they left the vixens to suckle their cubs and made their way out of the quarry.

The mist had now lifted. Looking down at the Island of Cats, Black Tip grumbled, 'I know one animal I'm not going to ask.'

Fang smiled. 'Sure if it keeps them happy, what's the harm in it?'

'And you know,' said Skulking Dog, 'Vickey's right. If we could delay it just a little while, we might be able to manage.'

'Anyway,' added Hop-along, 'whoever's going to do the digging, it's not going to be me, so we better start asking.'

In spite of what he had said, Hop-along felt very silly putting his nose to a hole in a ditch and talking to a rat. His instinct was to try and frighten him out so that he could eat him. However, he restrained himself and put Vickey's proposition.

'If the dam is so big,' replied the rat, 'what can we do to help?'

'The more there are of us, the more damage we can do,' explained Hop-along.

'How do we know you won't kill us?' asked the rat.

Hop-along assured him that they wouldn't.

'But if you won't fall upon us,' said the rat, 'what about our other enemy, the stoat?'

Hop-along promised to see what he could do, and continued along the ditch until he came to a rabbit burrow. The rabbits, he found, were even more suspicious.

'How often foxes have fooled us before,' said a voice from the darkness of the burrow. 'Would we not be leaving our homes only to end up on the jaws of our greatest enemy?'

'If the rat is prepared to trust us, will you

not trust us too?' asked Hop-along.

'It is more difficult for us,' said the rabbit. 'And even if we do, would we be safe from the stoat and the badger?'

'We hope to get their help too,' Hop-along replied.

'And what about the otters?' asked the rabbit. 'We cannot go to the lake unless they agree.'

'We'll talk to all the animals,' Hop-along assured him.

'All right, answered the rabbit. 'If you have their help, then you have ours. But remember, all must agree. To us one enemy is as bad as three.'

Black Tip meanwhile, had come across a stoat hunting along a dry stone wall. Small though this animal was, he knew it to be a clever and fearless fighter. He also knew stoats sometimes hunted in packs, and it occurred to him that if they banded together they could be of great help.

The stoat laughed when he heard what Black Tip had to say.

'But we have much in common,' argued Black Tip.

'The only thing we have in common,' said the stoat, 'is the black tip on our tails, and even that is most uncommon in foxes.'

'Do we not hunt the same way, eat the same food, even use the same tricks?'

'But what help would we be? We don't dig.

We don't need to.'

'You could if you wished,' said Black Tip. 'And after all, we are not your enemy. Man is your enemy.'

'We do not fear man,' asserted the stoat.

Black Tip knew this to be true. 'Still,' he added, 'if he floods the valley, he will drive away your food and you will have to find a new hunting ground.'

For all his ferocity, the stoat is also very intelligent, so he replied, 'Well, I suppose if the other animals agree, so will we.'

As things would have it, it fell to Fang to approach the badgers. He thought about it for a while before plucking up the courage. He was well aware that badgers are not only great diggers but powerful fighters and he had no wish to tangle with them. He had been booted out of a set once before, and this time he decided to keep his distance. A sharp bark would be enough to bring out the boar, he thought, and there would be ample opportunity to run if he turned out to be too unfriendly.

There was no response to the first bark, so he gave another, then a triple bark. A few moments later he saw a pointed snout poking up from behind the mound of earth at the entrance to the set, and a black and white striped head looked around to see what all the commotion was about. Fang knew the badger might not even see him, as his sight wasn't good, but that his sharp sense of smell would soon locate him.

The sniffing snout did its work, and the badger growled: 'Well, what do you want?'

Fang rose to his feet. 'I've come to seek your help.'

'Help,' laughed the badger. 'That's a good one. Foxes cause us more trouble than any other animals I know. You kill the hens and ducks and we get the blame. Why should we help you?'

'Because the valley is going to be flooded,' Fang told him. 'We need your help to attack the dam.'

The badger realised that if the valley was going to be flooded, he and his family would be in danger. Like the foxes, this was also their breeding time and at that very moment, in the depths of the set, his sow was suckling three cubs. At the same time, he knew the fox was clever and suspected he might be trying to use him. 'Are you sure you just don't want us to do your digging for you?' he asked Fang.

Fang knew the badger's suspicions were well founded. 'It's true,' he admitted, 'we don't like digging. That's why we use your sets when we find them empty. But really, the valley is in great danger, so we need your help and the help of all animals. Even if we could only delay the dam just long enough to rear our young.'

'But will the other animals agree?' asked the badger. 'How will you get them to work with their enemies?'

'Enemies we may be,' replied Fang, 'but if we don't agree to work together we will all lose to our greatest enemy – man.'

'All right,' said the badger at last, 'but you and all the others must do your share.'

Skulking Dog searched the lake shore for otters but in vain. Their scent was there all right. It was quite unmistakable. But then, so was Ratwiddle's. Realising that Ratwiddle's presence had probably frightened them off, he returned to the quarry.

Vickey and Sinnéad listened as, one by one, the dog foxes reported back.

'So it all depends on the otters,' said Vickey. 'What do you think Black Tip, will the otters help?'

'It's hard to say,' her mate replied. 'If it was Whiskers there'd be no problem. But I'd say he's gone back to the pheasant farm.'

'What do you think Skulking Dog?' asked Sinnéad.

Skulking Dog shook his head. 'I just don't know. I couldn't make any contact with them at all. It's my guess they're lying up in their holts until gloomglow.'

'Gloomglow it is then,' said Vickey, 'and let's hope they say yes.'

When darkness fell and the moon came up, Skulking Dog went down to the lake

155

again. For a long time he lay and listened to the sounds of the lake. He heard a scurry here, a plop there, and his instinct was to hunt. But he didn't move. After a while he saw what looked like two waterhens swimming towards him. Again he overcame the urge to rise and, to his surprise, found that what he was watching was an otter.

Skulking Dog now proceeded to put to the otter the same proposition that the others had put to the rat, the rabbit, the stoat and the badger. The response, however, was not the same.

'Why should we help you destroy the dam?' asked the otter from the darkness of the water.

'Why not?' asked Skulking Dog. 'If we don't destroy it, it will destroy us.'

'You perhaps,' grinned the otter, 'not us. We have nothing to fear from water. The more there is of it, the better we like it.'

'But it will drive our food away,' argued Skulking Dog. 'The mice, the rats, the rabbits and birds.'

'But the frogs, the fish and the waterhens will multiply,' said the otter.

'Will you not help us then?'

The otter turned to go. 'We have no reason to help you, but if you can think of some reason why we should, then we will.'

THIRTEEN

All the King's Horses

A large buff-tailed bumble bee whirred around the willow trees collecting pollen. At the far end of the valley the large yellow machines roared into life again after the Easter holiday. Far removed from their activity, Needle Nine watched Willow mending her tree house among the bushes from which she had taken her name. Her cousin Brian was standing in the shallow water in his wellingtons, handing her up the materials she needed.

'What's the point in building a tree house if the valley is going to be flooded?' he was asking.

'Because Grandad says we're to act as if nothing has happened,' Willow told him. 'He says we're not leaving and no one can make us.'

'But how can you stay?' asked the boy.

Willow shrugged her shoulders. 'I don't know, but he says he's not going.'

'And what does your father say?'

'He doesn't want to leave either. He'll lose some of his best sheep land.'

157

'What sort of sheep are they?'

'Wicklow Mountain Cheviots. Dad says they were brought over by Cromwell's soldiers. Some of the soldiers settled here and they brought the sheep from the Cheviot Hills between England and Scotland. That's why Dad still goes to Hawick sales in Scotland to buy rams.'

'I didn't think he would let you keep a fox,' said Brian. 'I mean, the way they attack sheep and everything.'

'He says they're not as bad as they're made out to be. But still, he keeps a sharp eye on the lambs, and he makes me keep a close eye on Needle Nine. Isn't that right Needle Nine?'

Willow looked around, but Needle Nine was gone. She smiled mischievously. 'He'd kill me if he knew I was letting Needle Nine run around on his own.' Then she added, 'He's not the first fox we've had you know.'

'I never knew you had another one,' said Brian. 'How did you get it?'

'Well it's funny the way it happened,' Willow told him. 'You see, there's a trapper at the other end of the valley, and he snares a lot. One day we found this fox caught in a snare he had set, down near the lake. It was half-dead and was being attacked by rats. We brought it home and put it in a pen, but we couldn't keep it. I don't know whether it was because of the rats or the snare, but it

158

was very wild, you know, sort of frightened, so we had to let it go. We still see it sometimes down by the lake. The snare has left it with a stiff neck, and it's still wearing the red dog collar we had on it. Dad calls it Ratcatcher. He thinks it's a bit mad.'

'Poor thing,' said Brian, 'but at least it's still alive.'

Willow helped her cousin up into the tree house, saying, 'We've also got peregrine falcons up on the mountain. Dad says they're very rare. Maybe we'll go up later and see if we can spot them.' She fixed another board into place before adding, 'There are also four cats marooned on the island. I must ask Dad to help us get them off.'

When the machines burst into life again, they sent a shiver through the valley. Perhaps it was because they had been silent for several days. More likely it was because word of what was happening had spread like wildfire, and the creatures who heard them now knew what they were doing. The mouse dropped the leaves she was using to line her nest and scuttled deeper into the ditch. The rat cocked an ear and dashed into the nearest drain. The hedgehog rolled up into a tight ball. The rabbit twitched his ears towards the sound and promptly disappeared into his warren. The stoat dropped the dead bird he was carrying, picked it up again and bounded in among the stones. The badger raised his small white-tipped ears above the mound of brown earth, sniffed the wind for scent of danger, and dived back into his set. Even the otter, asleep in the depths of his holt, felt the tremor of the earth and took to the water.

Hearing the machines, the dog foxes discontinued hunting and returned to the quarry. The vixens were visibly agitated and every now and then dashed up to the rim of the quarry to look down the valley.

'Here's Needle Nine,' said Fang.

Needle Nine was speeding up through the fields, and was almost out of breath when he reached them. 'It's the dam,' he gasped. 'They've started working on it again.'

Black Tip nodded. 'We hear them.'

'I think they're going to finish it,' said Needle Nine.

Hop-along arrived now too, and asked, 'What are we going to do?'

'If only we had the otters to help us,' said Vickey.

'They would, if we could give them a reason,' said Skulking Dog.

'There's one otter who has reason to help us,' Hop-along reminded them.

'Whiskers,' said Sinnéad, 'but he's probably back at the pheasant farm.'

'If that's where he is,' said Fang, 'I'll find him.'

A lark hovered high in the sky, so high it was almost hidden in the sun, but down in the valley its song could be heard, clear and beautiful above the noise of man's machines. It was almost as if nature was rising above what man was trying to do and saying it couldn't be allowed to happen. The machines, however, said something else. They were the tools man used to make things happen, to change the face of the fields and alter the very order of life.

Below the mountain, Willow's father checked a fresh crop of new-born lambs. He glanced up at the lark. Even if it survived the falcons, he knew it wouldn't sing for long. He looked down the valley towards the glistening white dam and the yellow machines that moved around it like ants. The noise of the machines was a constant reminder that his way of life was threatened too. Determined as he was to resist the project and stay in the valley, the machines told him quite clearly that he was fighting a losing battle. Just how long he and his neighbours could ignore them was uncertain. He looked at the lake. The thought of it swelling up to engulf his farmstead and his fields was something he found difficult to accept.

Whatever about him, he knew it would break the hearts of the old folk. Farming had brought him prosperity and provided him with a new bungalow higher up the valley that he was planning to move to anyway. That at least was some consolation. It was different for the old folk. Their roots were in their cottage. It was there they had started out in life. It was there their children had been born. It was from there their family had set out, some to America, one to stay and work the farm. If the water forced the old folk to leave, they'd be leaving more than a cottage behind them. He turned and looked up at the mountain. As a boy he had often heard them tell stories of how the foxes had helped to save the valley in times of trouble, but he knew it would take more than superstition to save it now.

From the rim of the quarry opposite, Vickey lay and watched the farmer. She too listened to the lark and the sound of man's machines. She looked up at the mountain and thought about Old Sage Brush and what he had told them. Somehow she knew that whatever the great god Vulpes had intended, the foxes would have to look after themselves.

Whiskers sat back on his tail and uttered his familiar flute-like whistle. 'What a dam!' he exclaimed. 'I didn't realise it was so big.'

'Can you help us?' asked Fang.

Whiskers was still mesmerised by the sheer size of the dam that confronted them.

'I hope so,' he said.

'Do you think we can do it?' asked Fang.

'I don't know. I've never seen anything as big as that before.'

'But if all the animals of the valley join us, maybe we can do it,' urged Black Tip.

'Maybe,' said Whiskers. 'Maybe, I don't know... But I suppose it's worth a try.'

'What about the other otters?' asked Skulking Dog. 'Do you think you can get them to help us too?'

Whiskers smiled. 'Don't you worry about the other otters. Just leave them to me.'

As the foxes returned to Beech Paw, Whiskers made his way up the river and into the lake. He wasn't long in searching out the otter holts under the Island of Cats and quickly summoned a meeting.

After hearing what he had to say, the otter who had spoken to Skulking Dog sat up and said, 'But what reason would we have for destroying the dam?'

'The foxes helped me when I was destroying a dam,' Whiskers replied, and he went on to tell them what had happened at the pheasant farm when it was being raided by a greedy mink and he was getting the blame.

'But that's no reason why we should help them to destroy this dam,' said another, a bitch otter.

'That's right,' said the first otter. 'We have

nothing to fear from water. The more there is of it, the more we enjoy it.'

Now Whiskers knew from what the foxes had told him that these were the arguments the lake otters would make. However, he knew something that the foxes didn't know and that was that otter cubs don't learn to swim until their fur is waterproof. So he said, 'True, *you* have nothing to fear from water, but some of you must have young.'

'I have a litter,' said the bitch otter.

'And I,' said another.

'And when your holts are flooded,' said Whiskers, 'where are you going to care for them until they are ready to be taught the ways of the water.'

'Mine have already been taught the ways of the water,' said the first bitch.

'Mine aren't old enough,' said the second.

'Nor mine,' said a third. 'What will we do?'

'Well, to be truthful,' Whiskers told them, 'I don't think the foxes really expect to *destroy* the dam. But if you could help them to *delay* it, you might have time to show your cubs the ways of the water before the flood comes. Then you could all enjoy it.'

It was coming on to dusk when Whiskers arrived at the quarry. He brought the foxes the good news that the otters had agreed to help them. Now all they had to do was tell the rest of the animals and convince them they had nothing to fear.

When the moon was lighting up the valley, and the sounds of man had finally died away, Black Tip took his mate up into the evergreens. Sinnéad had agreed to mind the cubs so that the honour of launching the attack on the dam could fall to Vickey. Moments later, the shriek of the she fox shattered the stillness of the night.

There was silence, and Vickey whispered, 'I hope they come.'

Black Tip hoped so too, and together they waited. For a while it seemed that Vickey's call had gone unanswered. Then their sharp ears detected a furtive dart here, a scurry there, first from one direction, then another, and almost before they knew it, a great rushing noise filled the night, a noise like a forest of leaves rustling in the wind, and they realised that a multitude of creatures were converging on the evergreens. Shadows turned into shapes, and soon, it seemed, all the animals of the valley had come and were carpeting the pine needles with their furry bodies. Perhaps the smaller ones felt there was safety in numbers. Who knows? But those who hunted so hard for so few, were amazed to see so many. Small eyes glinted in anxious glances and there were uneasy shufflings and whisperings, especially among those who found themselves too close to the stoats and foxes for comfort. However, all stood their ground until once more Vickey raised her head and screamed into the night.

For many of those gathered under the evergreens, it was a scream that had often sent a chill of fear down their spines, and even before it died away it spurred them into action. Suddenly the moonlit fields became a sea of movement as thousands of mice, rats, rabbits, hedgehogs, stoats, otters, badgers and foxes raced to the dam. Not even the foxes had ever seen anything like it before. It had the proportion of a flight from a forest fire, or the rush of lemmings to the sea.

Vickey insisted on going too and, when she arrived some time later with Black Tip, the work was well under way. Along the entire length of the dam a horde of animals of all shapes and sizes were digging furiously into the foundations. Black Tip joined them. On one side of him was a badger. On the other a rabbit. For once all enmity was gone as they scraped and dug against the enemy that was common to them all.

After some time, Whiskers came up to where Vickey waited near the small beech wood.

'Well,' she asked anxiously.

'The foundations are deep,' the otter told her.

'Then we must dig deeper,' she said.

Throughout the night, the digging continued, and every now and then Whiskers came up to report to Vickey.

'I have never seen anything so deep,' he told her.

'Nor I,' said Black Tip, who had come up to join them. 'No matter how deep we dig, we come to a solid wall.'

'Can we go deeper?' asked Vickey.

'I don't know,' said Whiskers. 'We can try.'

Deeper and deeper the animals dug, but each time they found that man and his machines had dug even deeper.

'Not even a crack?' asked Vickey.

'Not even a crack,' said Whiskers.

Soon the first rays of dawn were streaking into the sky, and the animals began to drift away. They had done their work and they knew they must be home before daybreak.

'Tell me Black Tip,' said Vickey, 'do you think we have done it?'

'It's difficult to say,' he told her. 'We have done a lot of digging, but I don't know whether we've done any damage.'

'Only man will know that,' said Whiskers, 'and today will tell the tale.'

FOURTEEN

The Hunters and the Hunted

Glensinna was silent. No roar of a thousand horsepower disturbed the stillness. Other sounds, however, could be heard by anyone who cared to listen – the trill of the lark, the call of the curlew, the song of the thrush in the spindle tree. Those glensfolk who were still left came out of their houses to listen and wonder why the machines hadn't started. Willow and her cousin Brian set off for the dam to investigate, and Needle Nine went with them.

Up at Beech Paw, the foxes listened for the sound of the machines and, when it didn't come, Vickey asked, 'Well, what do you think?'

'I don't know,' said Black Tip. 'But I know you really started something last night, didn't you?'

Vickey smiled. 'It really was great, wasn't it? Everyone came to help us.'

'Everyone except Old Sage Brush,' said Skulking Dog.

'He must have had a reason,' said Sinnéad. She wrapped her brush around little Twinkle to keep her from straying and pulled her into her warm underside. 'How's She-la?' she asked Vickey.

'Her time's very near now. But it still doesn't keep her from going after frogs. Funny the way it works, isn't it?'

'She's gone off to the meadows again this morning,' Black Tip told them. 'Poor Hop-along. He can't watch her. She's always slipping off when he isn't looking.'

'Where's Whiskers?' asked Vickey.

'He went to the lake when the digging stopped,' said Fang. 'He said he'd wait to see whether we had done enough damage before going back to the pheasant farm.'

'He must be tired after the dig,' said Vickey. 'And so must you all. Better get some sleep while you can.'

In the small beech wood beside the dam, the rooks swayed in the upper-most branches and watched the groups of men examining the mounds of fresh brown soil and discussing what had been responsible.

'Must have been the glensfolk,' said one.

'I knew they'd make their move sooner or later,' said another.

'That's not the work of people,' said a third man. 'That's the work of animals.'

'How can it be the work of animals?' asked the first man. 'All the animals in the world couldn't cause as much damage as that.'

169

'There'd have to be an awful lot of them all right,' said the second man. 'Look, it's right along the entire length of the dam.'

'Foxes,' said the third man. 'And badgers. And maybe rabbits as well.'

The other two men laughed.

'Who ever heard of rabbits and badgers digging in the same place?' said the first man.

'Or rabbits and foxes?' added the second.

'Why not?' asked the third. 'Don't rabbits and foxes sometimes live in a badger set, even when there are badgers in it? And don't forget, this is Glensinna.'

'So what?' asked the other men.

'Glensinna,' explained the third man. 'The Valley of the Fox.'

As the other two now examined the diggings more closely, they could indeed see traces of animals, and they realised this wasn't the work of man. At the same time, they couldn't imagine that animals were capable of causing damage on such a scale, so they looked up the valley and wondered about it.

Farther along the dam, the foreman and site engineer examined the damage.

'Well?' asked the foreman. 'Have the foundations been damaged?'

'I doubt it,' said the engineer. 'But I'll have to carry out some tests to make sure. It depends on how deep these holes go, whether they go down under the foundations.'

'It must have taken a lot of vermin to do that,' observed the foreman.

'How are you going to keep them away tonight?' asked the engineer.

The foreman pushed back his cap and scratched his head. 'Unless we put down poison. Or bring in some dogs.'

'Well, you'll have to do something,' the engineer told him, 'or we'll all be out of a job.'

Turning around, the foreman spotted Needle Nine who was standing not far from Willow, sniffing the scents the other animals had left. 'Look,' he shouted, 'there's one of them.'

Needle Nine looked up in time to see the foreman picking up a large stone and hurling it in his direction.

'No,' cried Willow, 'he's just a pet.'

Her cry fell on deaf ears. The workmen, who were uncertain now as to whether they were going to have any work, followed the foreman's example, picking up stones and running towards the fox.

'Run Needle Nine, run!' cried Willow.

Needle Nine needed no bidding. As the first stone whizzed past his head, he wheeled around and streaked towards the beech wood. A shower of stones sailed after him and he dived for cover.

'Come on Brian,' said Willow, 'let's tell Dad.'

Up at Beech Paw, the vixens suckled their cubs and dozed. Nearby, the dog foxes were still asleep after their exertions of the night. On the rim of the quarry, Hop-along, who hadn't been digging, lay and kept watch. Elsewhere in the valley, the badgers snored deep in their sets, the rabbits hunched up and nibbled the grass, the rats and mice went their secretive ways as if nothing had happened, while down in the lake the otters curled around their young and rested.

Suddenly a shot rang out. Then another and another. The smaller animals ran for cover. The larger animals awoke with a start and dashed out to see where the danger was. Black Tip was at Hop-along's side in an instant, followed by Fang and Skulking Dog.

'Where's it coming from?' asked Black Tip.

'The meadows,' said Hop-along, 'and She-la's down there hunting frogs. I must go to her.'

As Hop-along hobbled off down the hillside, Fang told the others, 'You two stay here. I'll go with him.'

Not knowing what was happening, Vickey and Sinnéad were getting ready to pick up their cubs and seek refuge in the black-thorns.

'No need to go yet,' Skulking Dog told

them. 'The shooting's down in the meadows. If it comes any closer we can go to earth.'

Above the mountain, the two falcons were circling ever higher in a graceful dance of courtship when they heard the shooting and soared away up the valley. Down at the farm, Willow and her cousin dashed out of the house and ran across the fields.

'It's the men from the dam,' she cried. 'They're shooting all the animals.'

In fact, the shooters included only a few of the workers. Most of them were hunters the foreman had brought to the valley. Vermin, he vowed, couldn't be allowed to hold up work on the dam.

The glensfolk, however, took a different view. They had no liking for the people who were building the dam, so they ordered the hunters to leave.

'You no longer own this land,' protested the foreman.

'Maybe not,' said Willow's father, 'but we're still living here, and so long as we do, there'll be no shooting in Glensinna.'

'Look,' said the boy, 'they've already killed some of the animals.'

'A fox,' said Willow's father.

'And good riddance,' said the foreman as the hunters turned to go.

'It's a vixen,' cried Willow. 'A pregnant vixen.'

'So it is,' said another farmer. 'Well, it could have been worse.'

The two farmers lifted the vixen and left her in the grass at the foot of the nearest hedge.

'Come on Willow,' said her father. 'There's nothing more we can do.'

The two men walked off home, and Willow knelt beside the body of the vixen. 'Look Brian,' she cried. 'She's not dead.' Willow ran her fingers over the soft fur, saying, 'She's been hit around the head.' She thought for a moment. 'I wonder if she's one of the foxes I saw up at the blackthorns?'

From the cover of the hedge on the far side of the field, Hop-along and Fang watched the two young people lift the limp body of She-la and carry her up the valley. There was nothing they could do but follow at a safe distance.

'She's heavy,' panted the boy. He was holding the back legs, Willow the front ones, and the fine pointed head hung back almost to the ground, smearing the green grass red as it passed.

'I must leave her down for a moment,' said Brian.

'Me too,' gasped Willow. 'I never thought a fox could be so heavy.' She placed her hand on where she presumed the vixen's heart to be, and said, 'She's still breathing. Come on, let's get her back up to the earth.'

Bit by bit they lugged the limp body of She-la up the side of the valley. They rested at the fallen ash, again at the large chestnut tree, the big brown buds of which were now beginning to open. Finally, feeling warm and tired and out of breath, they reached the blackthorns and laid the fox down near the entrance to the earth.

'We don't want to go too close,' said Willow, 'or we might frighten the others away.'

'Do you think it'll do any good?' asked Brian. 'I mean, leaving her here like that?'

'I don't know,' replied Willow. 'Maybe the others can do something for her. I just don't know.'

It was some time later before any of the other foxes ventured near She-la.

Hop-along was the first to hobble over. First he sniffed, then he announced: 'She's alive Fang, she's alive!'

Vickey and Sinnéad were beside them now too. Gently Fang helped Hop-along to pull She-la towards the earth while the two vixens nudged and pushed and helped in every way they could. Once she was at the entrance, it was easier to pull her the rest of the way down.

'Where will we put her?' asked Hop-along.

'In her own place,' said Sinnéad.

Together they manoeuvred her into the little side chamber she had prepared so carefully for the arrival of her cubs.

175

'Now we must see to her wound,' said Vickey

She-la had taken the shot in the region of her skull, and this had probably saved her life. The pellets had penetrated the skin, but not the bone, and she was now suffering from the condition man would call concussion.

While Black Tip and Skulking Dog waited at the quarry and kept watch over the cubs, Vickey and Sinnéad now set about the task of cleaning She-la's wound and searching for any other pellets that might have strayed into her body. They had done it often before and knew what to look for.

'Well?' asked Hop-along when they had finished. 'How is she?'

'She's alive,' said Vickey.

'But will she live?' he asked.

'We don't know,' Sinnéad told him. 'She's still asleep.'

'What about her unborn cubs?' asked Hop-along.

'Only Vulpes can tell,' said Vickey. 'Let her rest now. We've done all we can for her.'

Returning to the quarry, Vickey now reproached herself for what had happened to She-la. Talking to the others, she told them she felt she was to blame.

'How were you to know the shooters would come after us?' said Sinnéad.

'That's right,' said Black Tip. 'How were

you to know? How were any of us to know?'

'And anyway,' said Skulking Dog, 'the attack on the dam was a great idea. I've never seen anything like it in my life.'

'Nor any of us,' Black Tip told her. 'No other fox would have thought of getting the other animals to help us.'

'I'll never forget the way they dug into the foundations of the dam,' said Fang. 'It was really great.'

'But was it?' asked Vickey. 'Was it worth the effort? Was it worth She-la's life? The dam still stands.'

'Of course it was worth the effort,' said Hop-along, who had arrived to hear what Vickey was saying. 'The shooters wouldn't have come after us if we hadn't done a lot of damage.'

'And don't forget,' said Black Tip, 'the people on the farm came to our aid. That's what you'd expect in the Land of Sinna, isn't it?'

'Maybe so,' sighed Vickey, 'but even the Land of Sinna isn't worth She-la's life and the life of her cubs.'

Vickey, however, had spoken too soon. That night, mother nature worked a miracle in the Land of Sinna. Unconscious though she was, She-la gave birth to four fine cubs. Man might say it couldn't happen, but then nature has many secrets that even man doesn't know.

Next morning, Hop-along's excitement knew no bounds. He was the father of four cubs. 'And they're not a bit like me,' he told the others. 'They've all got four legs!'

Black Tip could see that his spirits were as high as the lark in the sky. 'Congratulations!' He smiled. 'Vulpes has been good to you.'

'Indeed he has,' agreed Hop-along. 'All we need now is for She-la to get well.'

'How is she?' asked Fang.

'She still sleeps,' Hop-along told him.

'Then how will she look after her cubs?' asked Black Tip.

'She won't have to,' said Vickey. 'Sinnéad has agreed to take her cub up to the blackthorns. She'll take the den across from She-la and feed her cubs too until she's well.'

FIFTEEN

Danger at Gloomglow

Dark clouds shrouded the Mountain of Vulpes, and rain swept across the valley. Willow and her young cousin ran across the muddy yard and nipped into a row of outhouses beside the barn. Inside, her father and a farm worker were treating some lambs. Since the dam had begun to take shape, it seemed that nothing was going right. Sheep needed a lot of attention at any time, but lambing had been particularly difficult this year. Now several of the lambs were down with scour, a sort of diarrhoea. They wouldn't eat and without food they'd curl up and die. As the farm worker held up a lamb, Willow's father squirted penicillin down its throat with a plastic syringe and held its mouth closed to force it to swallow. The penicillin would dry up its stomach and help it to hold food again.

In the next stall, Willow fed another lamb with a special mixture from a bottle with a teat. By right this lamb shouldn't have been there at all. It had been a difficult birth. The lamb had lived but the ewe had died, and

Willow had taken the orphan under her care.

'Where's Needle Nine?' asked her father.

'I don't know,' she replied. 'I think he's up the yard somewhere.'

'Well, you want to keep an eye on him. Make sure he doesn't go near the sheep. We've enough trouble with them.'

'He hasn't bothered with the sheep Dad, not since the day we got him.'

'I know that, but still, it's in their nature, so just keep an eye on him.'

'Do you think it was the foxes that were at the dam?' Brian asked him.

'It's hard to say.'

'Grandad says it was,' said Willow. 'What do you think Dad?'

'I heard that said all right,' said her father. 'But it'll take more than foxes to stop the dam now.'

'Some people are talking of other action,' said his helper.

'Who?'

'Oh, you know, the boys. They say there's only one way to stop it.'

Willow's father squirted another dose of penicillin down a lamb's throat and held its mouth shut. 'What, you mean blow it up? And what good will that do? Sure the council will only build it again.'

'Maybe so,' said the helper, 'but that's the way they're talking.'

'We were down at the dam this morning,'

said Willow 'The foundations have been tested and I think the men are getting ready to start work again.'

'Better stay away from the dam from now on,' warned her father. 'If there's trouble brewing, you want to keep clear of it.'

While Willow may have thought that Needle Nine was somewhere in the yard, in fact he was up at the blackthorns with Hop-along, who was now grieving for his mate, his initial high spirits at becoming a father having given way to gloom.

'I was lucky to escape myself,' said Needle Nine, and told him how the men had stoned him.

Hop-along nodded. 'I'm glad you got away.'

'How are the cubs?'

'Fine. Sinnéad's looking after them.'

'No one else hurt?'

Hop-along shook his head. 'Just She-la.'

'Has she made any move at all?'

'Not a move. She just lies there. She's breathing, but she doesn't move.'

On the way back Needle Nine called in to the other foxes at the quarry. 'I followed Willow and the boy down towards the dam this morning,' he told them.

'Is the work still stopped?' asked Vickey.

Needle Nine lowered his head. 'I was afraid to go too close because they chased me with stones yesterday. But the men are back. I think they're getting ready to start again.'

'So we've failed to stop them?' said Vickey.

'It was worth a try,' consoled Needle Nine. 'And the other animals did their best.'

'We all did,' said Black Tip. 'But the question is, what do we do now?'

Even as they talked, the machines roared into life again.

It was still raining when Whiskers announced his arrival at the quarry with his usual whistle.

'They've started work on the dam again,' he told them.

'So I hear,' said Vickey sadly.

'I watched them from the river,' said the otter. 'The great yellow machines are filling in the holes we made.'

'It won't take them long,' remarked Black Tip.

'Maybe we should try again tonight,' suggested Whiskers.

'Whiskers,' said Vickey, 'you came here when we called on you for help. You convinced your fellow otters to join us. More than that we cannot ask.'

'If you want to mount another attack on the dam, you need only say the word,' offered Whiskers.

'I know,' said Vickey, 'and we all appreciate

what you say. But you see, who else would help us now?'

'It's true,' said Fang. 'The other animals won't help us again if the only result is to bring the shooters after them.'

'Then you must find another way,' urged Whiskers.

'What other way is there?' asked Skulking Dog. 'We've tried everything.'

'You'll think of something,' Whiskers assured them. 'Now, I must return to my own river. If you need any more help, you know where to find me.' So saying, he wished them well and left.

'You know,' said Vickey when he had gone, 'Whiskers is right. We must think of another way.'

'What else can we do?' asked Black Tip.

'I don't know,' confessed Vickey. 'All I know is that we must try. Needle Nine, you return to the farm and if man starts to move out, come and tell us. The rest of you can take turns watching the dam. We can't give up, not now.'

Hop-along continued to devote all his time to She-la. He had pulled some lacey leaves of cow parsley and pushed them under her injured head. Somehow he felt they would be soft and cool. As he lay and watched her lying there, motionless except for the faint rise and fall that told him she was still alive, he won-

dered if she would ever waken again. Would
she see the lovely cubs she had brought into
the Land of Sinna? Would she suckle them as
Sinnéad was now doing? But how, he wondered, could she live if she didn't eat? Then it
occurred to him that if she did wake up there
was no food for her. He'd have to hunt.

Leaving the valley behind him, he headed
up through the evergreens. Since She-la was
shot while hunting in the meadows, he
thought it better to keep out of the valley for
the moment. He came across the strong
scent of hare and followed it for some distance through the trees before he realised he
was wasting his time. Anyway, he said to
himself, what was a fox with three legs doing
following a hare? The thought amused him.
Farther along he spotted a rook that somehow had come to grief among the evergreens. It was hanging limply from the
withered branches of a tree that had fallen
against another. After several tries, he managed to keep his balance long enough to
climb up and get it. The rook had been dead
for some time, but he was hungry. He ate his
fill, then continued on through the evergreens in search of something for She-la.

Beyond the evergreens, Hop-along found
himself in an area of high gorse-covered
fields. A good place to hunt, he thought.
Plenty of cover and far from man. Trotting
into a secluded hollow, however, he suddenly

found himself face-to-face with several men sitting among the gorse. Startled, the men reached for their guns. Even more startled, Hop-along turned and ran as fast as he possibly could. With each faltering step he expected to hear the sound of shots. To his great surprise, none came.

Back in the hollow one of the men, a man with red hair, said, 'No need to worry. It's only a fox,' They all laughed and settled into their hiding place again to wait for darkness.

Having put a safe distance between himself and the shooters Hop-along paused to get his breath and decide what to do. Were they the ones who had wounded She-la he wondered. Perhaps coming at them from a different direction? Yet, if they were hunting, why hadn't they shot at him? Puzzled as he was, he realised his good fortune in having got out of the gorse alive, so he felt he must abandon his hunting expedition and return to warn the others.

In a ditch below the small beech wood, Fang lay and watched the men working at the dam. The great yellow machines had already filled in all the holes they had scraped and dug. Now there was nothing to tell that there had ever been any holes there. It had only taken a short time for the big silver blades to level the mounds of soft brown soil and for the giant wheels of other machines to pack the soil tightly in again. The dam itself remained as high and as solid as ever. How, he wondered, could they ever have hoped to damage such a dam? If Old Sage Brush could have seen it, would he have tried? Such thoughts were going through his mind when Black Tip arrived.

'Vickey asked me to warn you,' said Black Tip.

'About what?'

'Hop-along came across some shooters.'

'Where?'

'Up at the back of the evergreens.'

Fang looked back towards the beech wood. 'I didn't hear any shots.'

'There were none.'

'Strange.'

'That's what we all thought. Hop-along almost walked into them, but they didn't shoot.'

'Had they any fun dogs?'

Black Tip shook his head.

'Lucky for him,' said Fang.

'Vickey wants to see the dam for herself,' said Black Tip. 'I'll bring her down at gloomglow. It'll be safe enough then.'

'I'll be hunting myself by that time,' said Fang. 'Thanks for the warning.'

When man's machines had fallen silent once more, and the moon had crept into the sky to see what they had been doing, Black Tip led Vickey across the hillside. Skulking

Dog had agreed to stand guard at the quarry, and watch her cubs, while the others were safely tucked below ground up at the blackthorns. Vickey was still far from strong, but it was a nice night and she and Black Tip enjoyed a variety of scents as they made their way leisurely down through the fields.

Below them the lake gleamed in the light of gloom-glow and farther on they saw the lights of the old folk's cottage where they had lain and talked with Needle Nine. Beyond that, at the lower end of the lake were the lights of Willow's house where Needle Nine lived. They wondered what he was doing now.

The foxes weren't the only ones who were wondering what Needle Nine was doing. Willow and Brian had found that in spite of their precautions, the pet fox was nipping out of his pen in the middle of the night and going off. Where, they wondered, could he be going? They only hoped he wasn't going near any of the lambs. They weren't to know, of course, that he was making regular visits to the foxes up at Beech Paw. All they knew was that, when the sheep dogs started barking again for no apparent reason, it was probably him slipping off somewhere, so they decided to try and follow him. Dressing quickly, they got to the yard just in time to see him struggling out of his pen and going off towards the river. In fact, the little fox had decided to hunt, as his instinct told him he should, and then perhaps take something up to Hop-along and She-la.

'Where do you think he's going?' whispered Brian.

'I don't know,' replied Willow. 'He just seems to be poking around.'

Quietly they watched as the shadowy figure of Needle Nine nosed his way down-river. Then they lost him.

'Come on,' whispered Willow, 'let's see if we can find him.'

Holding hands, the two young people made their way across the moonlit meadows.

'It's hopeless,' said Brian at last. 'I can't see a thing.'

'We're almost at the dam,' said Willow. 'And look, there he is.'

Silhouetted against the white sloping side of the dam, they could see the familiar out-line of Needle Nine. Unknown to them, he had often come to the dam before in search of scraps of food left by the workmen.

'Come on,' said Willow, 'let's get him and take him back.'

Black Tip and Vickey were now on the hill-side above the small beech wood. They saw the two young people and Needle Nine meeting on the side of the dam. From where they were, they could also see a group of shadowy figures on the other side and, knowing Needle Nine had been attacked at the dam before, they feared he might be in danger.

'We must get him away from there,' said Vickey.

'Quick,' urged Black Tip. 'Call him.'

Immediately, Vickey raised her head and sent the weird cry of the she fox shrieking across the valley. Startled, the shadowy figures ran off. On the other side of the dam, Needle Nine ran towards the beech wood, and the two young people were left.

'It sounds like a banshee,' whispered Brian.

'That's no banshee,' said Willow. 'That's a vixen, and it's calling Needle Nine. Hurry, before we lose him.'

Hardly had the two young people reached the edge of the beech wood, than a huge explosion erupted in the middle of the dam. Turning, they saw a great orange flame shooting up into the night sky and then mushrooming outwards in a pall of heavy black smoke. At the same time, a shower of stones began to rain down on them. They covered their heads with their hands and ran for the shelter of the trees.

Up in the blackthorns, Hop-along dashed out to see what had happened, then almost immediately returned to make sure She-la was all right.

'Look,' exclaimed Sinnéad as he arrived beside her. 'Look, she's awake!'

So she was. The sound of the explosion had stirred within She-la's injured brain the memory of the shot that had brought her down, and the deep instinct of survival had roused her from her sleep.

SIXTEEN

Under the Mountain

The sun sparkled on the lake and almost blinded the amber eyes that watched from the reeds. Because of the explosion at the dam no further hunting had been done during the night, and Fang had now come to the lake shore in the hope that he might find a coot or even a waterhen. They were around somewhere, he knew. He could smell them. Perhaps they were in among the roots of the willows, where the slime webbed like a silvery frost. Then, he thought, the lake was for Ratwiddle and the otters, so he turned his attention to the old people's cottage on the side of the valley. He knew from the time Needle Nine had taken them there that the people had no dogs, and he wondered if they had any free-range chickens.

As Fang neared the cottage, he saw the old man lean on his stick and close the green half-door behind him. The old man walked slowly across the gravel and looked out over the lake at the mountain until the cry of children's voices attracted his attention. It was the boy and girl. The girl linked arms with her grandfather as they walked down the lane to the water's edge.

'Well, Willow my girl,' said the old man, 'time's running out.' He stopped for a moment to get his breath. 'What took you down to the dam last night?'

'We didn't get up to go to the dam,' she told him. 'We were looking for Needle Nine.'

'Even so, you must do what your father tells you, and stay away from it. That goes for you too, young Brian my lad.'

Brian, who was wading in the shallow water, nodded.

'It was the foxes that saved us, Grandad,' said Willow.

'So I hear,' said the old man. 'The whole valley's talking about it.'

'Do you think it was a sign?' asked Brian.

'Could be.'

'But do you think it was a good sign?' asked Willow.

The old man ruffled the girl's hair affectionately. 'It was if it saved you two from being blown up. The idiots. What do they expect to gain by that sort of thing?'

'I suppose they thought they might destroy the dam,' said Willow.

'And did they?'

Willow shook her head. 'They only blew a hole in the side of it. The men are fixing it now.'

'I thought as much,' said the old man. He

turned and looked across the lake at the mountain again. 'Time's running out...'

As often happens when people experience things they don't understand, the glensfolk had accepted the least likely explanation for the action of the foxes at the dam. In their own superstitious way, they were prepared to believe that the foxes had saved the lives of the two young people. It never occurred to them that the vixen wasn't warning Willow and Brian, but simply calling the other fox; In the same superstitious way, they had for generations, misinterpreted the movement of the foxes to the mountain in times of trouble.

She-la struggled to her feet and fell down again. The birth of her cubs, coming so soon after her injury, had left her very weak. She tried again and this time succeeded in staying on her feet. Rather shakily she made her way up out of the earth and dropped down on the soil at the entrance. The back of her head was very sore, but the blood had dried and the wound was healing. The sun seemed to pour new strength into her body, and if there was still a nip in the air she didn't notice.

Having adjusted her eyes to the brightness of the day, She-la looked out across the valley. The plaintive call of a curlew came to her ears. Two mallard rose from the lake and wheeled away down river into the wind. A snipe burst into flight and flashed its white underbelly to the sky before circling away across the mountain. She managed a smile. Some fox was hunting down there, and she wondered who. The song of a thrush brought her thoughts back from the meadows to her more immediate surroundings. It was somewhere along the blackthorns, which she could see were now beginning to blossom. She listened as it sang again. How beautiful, she thought. In a hawthorn tree, a chaffinch examined the new green leaves and ventured to taste them. Then it flitted down to a strand of barbed wire, plucked a few fox hairs off it, and flew away. She smiled again. It was so good to be alive.

She-la now felt well enough to eat, so Hop-along brought her back some frogs, only to find that her craving for frogs had gone. He didn't know whether to be sorry or glad, until it dawned on him that she was getting back to her old self again, and then he was glad. There was also great rejoicing among the other foxes at her recovery, a rejoicing surpassed only by the intense joy she herself had felt on seeing her four cubs for the first time. Already, the cubs were being encouraged by Sinnéad to suckle their mother and relieve her of the milk she had been storing for their arrival. A very happy Hop-along went out and brought in fresh leaves of cow parsley to line their den.

While the explosion had shattered She-la's sleep, the other foxes soon learned that it had not destroyed the dam. Black Tip reported that the great orange flame they had seen had torn a hole in the side of it. However, the dam still stood.

Vickey lay on the rim of the quarry looking across at the Mountain of Vulpes. Somehow, she thought, it seemed to be timeless, never changing. The billy-goat was there guarding the rocky slope as always, and the falcons were soaring high above the heather. But for them down in the valley, things were different. 'Time's running out,' she said to Black Tip.

Black Tip watched a blackbird balance precariously on the brambles across from where he lay and eye them with brief curiosity before screeching back up to the blackthorns. 'We'll have to move soon,' he said. 'The question is, where do we go?'

Fang had been watching a swan winging its way down the valley. Now, as it passed overhead with the familiar sound of the wind soughing through its great wings, he remarked: 'No need for it to go.'

'It's not going,' said Black Tip. 'It's coming.'

The swan circled around to the lake, skied along the surface for a moment, and settled gently into the water.

'Fang,' said Vickey, 'we must find Old

Sage Brush and warn him that the dam is nearing completion. When the flood comes his earth may be in danger too.'

'If it's on the lower slopes, it will be,' said Black Tip.

'If it's on the lower slopes, I'll find him,' said Fang.

Many of the hedges in Glensinna were now turning white as masses of small five-petalled blossoms spread tightly along the blackthorns. Down at the farm, slightly larger blossoms gave the plum bushes a similar appearance, so that they looked as if they had been accidentally covered with lime. Man wouldn't consider it summer for several more weeks, but nature has a calendar of its own.

Leaving a laneway lined with daffodils and primroses, Willow and Brian followed Needle Nine up to the lower slopes of the mountain. It was a long climb and several times they stopped to look back across the valley. Below them was the lake and the island, and Willow remarked that she must ask her father again about the cats. However, it was the falcons they were now going to see. Brian had never seen a falcon before and Willow was taking him up to show them to him.

Resuming their climb, they talked about the narrow escape they had had at the dam, and they knew they wouldn't be allowed to go there any more. Strictly speaking, they weren't allowed up on the mountain on their own either, but they felt that after what had happened at the dam, no one would mind.

Up and up they went, until at long last they were able to make their way across to the top of the rocky slope directly above the lake. The billy-goat got up at their approach and hopped on to an outcrop of rock where he stood and watched them.

'It's very steep, isn't it?' said Brian, looking down at the lake.

Willow nodded. 'And some of the stones are very loose. But if we're careful we can get down as far as the nest.'

They watched as Needle Nine nosed around. He found fresh droppings and knew they had been left by another dog fox to mark out his territory. Such markings, however, meant little to him. Once he was with Willow he could safely ignore them and always did. The scent indicated a fox path on the slope, so he stepped over on to it and began making his way down. Cautiously Willow and Brian followed. Stones rolled and slipped under their feet, dead branches broke as they reached out for support. Now and then a stone rolled right down to the bottom, and fell over the edge into the water. When that happened, they stopped to get a better foothold and scan the sky for the falcons.

There was no sign of them, so they

continued on down until they were level with the nest. It was perched precariously on a narrow ledge of rock and consisted of a large clump of twigs that were whitened with droppings. There were no eggs in it, so they looked around for Needle Nine.

'He's after another fox,' said Willow.

'How do you know?'

'Can't you smell it? It's an old dog fox.' Willow had often heard her grandfather talk of smelling an old dog fox, and assumed that if there was a smell of a fox it had to be a dog fox.

Brian sniffed, but he wasn't used to foxes and couldn't smell anything except the moss-covered stones and the rotting branches.

They lay back on the stones and craned their necks so that they could scan the slope from side to side. There was no sign of Needle Nine, so they edged themselves farther down.

'Careful,' warned Willow. 'We don't want to start another landslide. Remember what Grandad was telling us about the landslide that happened up here after the Night of the Big Wind?'

Brian remembered only too well and now, as he inched his way down after Willow, he could just imagine how the side of the mountain had collapsed with all the rain. 'Do you think we should go any farther?' he wondered.

'We can't go back up without Needle Nine,' said Willow. 'He may be stuck somewhere.'

Reaching a ledge a short distance above the lake, they could now see there were holes under several outcrops of rock. Realising that Needle Nine could have gone into any one of them, Willow crawled over to the nearest and called him. There was no response.

Brian edged over beside her. 'Is this a fox's earth?'

'I'd say it's being used by a fox all right. Can't you smell him?'

Brian shook his head. 'All I can hear is running water.'

Willow cocked her ear to the opening and listened. 'You're right. It must be an underground river. I hope Needle Nine can find his way out.'

'Look,' cried Brian, 'there he is, up there.'

The little fox had emerged from under the rocks a short distance above them. Delighted to see him, they scrambled up to him, then bit by bit, climbed back up to the top. As they sat down to get their breath, the falcons appeared, soaring past with wings locked, glaring at the intruders. They couldn't have asked for a better view of the birds, but Willow feared that their presence might cause them to desert the nest, so after a short time they made their way back down to the valley.

The old man was sitting in front of the cottage when the children arrived and told him about their visit to the mountain.

'Fox earths, you say?'

The children nodded.

'And an underground river,' added Willow.

The old man looked across at the mountain, saying softly to himself, 'The Night of the Big Wind.'

'Do you think it was caused by the landslide?' asked Willow.

The old man nodded. 'Must have been.'

'Do you think it could have formed caves in there too?' asked Brian. 'The river sounded very deep down.'

'I wouldn't be surprised.'

'But Grandad,' said Willow, 'you know what I was thinking?'

'What?'

'If there's an underground river there, how will the valley hold water?'

The old man, who was still looking across at the mountain, smiled. 'You know,' he said, 'that's just what I was wondering.'

'The men at the dam won't believe it when we tell them,' said Willow. 'Do you think we should?'

'Should what?' asked the old man almost absentmindedly.

'Tell them?'

The old man smiled again. 'Now why

should we tell them if they won't believe it? Let's say it's our secret. Ours and the foxes.'

Failing to locate Old Sage Brush on the lower slopes, Fang returned to the quarry. Even as he was informing the others, Needle Nine arrived to tell them what he had found on the mountain.

'So that's where he is,' said Fang. 'Little wonder I couldn't find him.'

'Well, we can find him now,' said Skulking Dog. 'I'll go this time.'

Vickey shook her head. 'No, I'll go. If anybody's going to tell him that it's time to move, I think it should be me.'

'But you can't,' protested Black Tip. 'You're not strong enough.'

'And the great hunting birds were very annoyed with us,' warned Needle Nine. 'If they attack, you might lose your footing.'

Vickey, however, was adamant. 'Black Tip,' she said, 'you can come with me. Skulking Dog, if you could put up the grouse, that would draw off the hunting birds. And Fang, you're tired now, perhaps you could stay here and watch over the cubs.'

Seeing that she had made up her mind, and knowing the great affection she had for the old fox, the others reluctantly agreed.

As it turned out, Vickey had studied the falcons well during the days she was confined to the quarry. She knew they had a particular liking for the red grouse. When Skulking Dog flushed them from the heather, she and Black Tip were able to make their way down to the ledge above the lake without interference. For a moment they looked across at Beech Paw and wondered if the others could see them. Then they turned and, following the familiar scent of Old Sage Brush, disappeared under a nearby rock.

Even though he was blind, and the sound of falling water must have dulled his hearing, the old fox was waiting for them just inside. They wondered how he knew they were coming, but he didn't say. As he led them deeper into the mountain, he merely warned, 'Be careful how you tread. The paths are narrow and the crevices are deep.'

'How do you know where you are going?' asked Black Tip after a while.

'In here,' said the old fox. 'I can see as well as you, maybe better.'

Coming to a cave where the floor was dry and the sound of water a distant echo, Old Sage Brush lay down, saying, 'You must be tired, Vickey. I told you not to come.'

'She wanted to warn you,' said Black Tip. 'The dam will soon be finished, and you too will be in danger.'

The old fox smiled. 'It will not be the first time the fox has been in danger. That is why Vulpes caused a great wind to blow and created this earth. It has given us refuge many times. It enabled us to survive when a great fire burned in the valley.'

'But what about the flood?' asked Vickey anxiously. 'Will it give us refuge from that?'

Old Sage Brush shook his head, saying, 'This earth will no longer be dry.'

'You mean it'll be flooded?' asked Black Tip.

Once more the old fox shook his head. 'How can it be flooded if it cannot hold water? It will serve the fox again, but not in the way it has in the past. Listen and you will understand.'

As they listened, they heard again the sound of running water far below them. And in that moment they realised what the old fox was telling them. When the water rose, it would flow into this earth. But it would rise no farther. For somewhere under the mountain it would flow away again.

'Sage Brush,' said Vickey, 'we have misjudged you. You told us before that our earths would stay dry, and we did not believe you. You must forgive us.'

Old Sage Brush smiled. 'Vickey,' he said, 'you can see further then most. But even you cannot expect to see everything. Come now, I must take you back out of the mountain. There are many ways to come here and many ways to go, and not all of them as difficult as the one you have found.'

SEVENTEEN

Twins of the Wise

A far-off bark and the sound of children at play came to the ears of the foxes up at Beech Paw. They knew it was Needle Nine and the two young people in the fields near the old folk's cottage. The old people had moved out when the dam was completed, but now they were back. To everyone's surprise, they had been the first to move. There were those who believed that they must have had another sign, for it was widely rumoured that the foxes had been seen on the mountain. Whatever it was, the old folk had decided to leave, and for some reason hadn't seemed too unhappy about it. The others had followed, taking their cattle and sheep, dogs and cats. They had even removed the cats from the island, and taken them with them.

Later, the glensfolk had gathered to see their valley being flooded. And, although they may not have known it, the wild animals had watched too, for few of *them* had to move, apart from the otters, and they didn't have to go very far. They had seen the water rising to cover the reeds. It had covered the willows and the Island of Cats. It had covered the farm house and the outbuildings. It had covered the trapper's cottage and the shed containing the snares and traps. However, it hadn't risen as far as the blackthorns or the quarry. It hadn't even gone up as far as the old people's cottage. For some strange reason, it wouldn't rise beyond a certain point on the rocky slope across on the mountain. The foxes knew why, of course. The old folk knew, and so did the children, but they weren't telling anyone.

The rest of the people of Glensinna didn't quite know why the water refused to rise any farther. However, they did know it was something to do with the foxes. As a result the foolish superstition that the foxes had once again saved Glensinna, or at least a large part of it, reigned supreme.

Beneath the beeches, Vickey and Black Tip lay and watched their cubs at play. The hard buds of the beech had finally burst, allowing the leaves to break the silvery threads that seemed to bind them, and emerge as soft and delicate as butterflies' wings.

Little Black Tip and Running Fox rolled and pounced and chased their tails. They approached a bumble bee that was collecting nectar from the flowers, nudged it and ran up the bank between the trees. In their excitement, the flight from the bee developed into a chase, of what, neither Black Tip nor Vickey could imagine.

They smiled. It was nice to see the cubs coming on so well. Soon they'd have to think of taking them out and showing them how to hunt. No doubt, Old Sage Brush would help Skulking Dog and Sinnéad to train Twinkle, and Hop-along might need some assistance when it came to showing She-la's cubs the ways of the wild. Fang would help too, if he was still around. Ratwiddle might even have something to tell them, provided he could be persuaded to get rid of his fleas. For as Old Sage Brush was quick to point out, they all needed each other, and sometimes the fool was the twin of the wise.

And so, things returned to normal in Glensinna. The hedgehog was hunting the mouse again. The stoat was hunting the rat and the rabbit. The fox was hunting them all, but for the time being at any rate, man had ceased to hunt the fox.

The publishers hope that this book has given you enjoyable reading. Large Print Books are especially designed to be as easy to see and hold as possible. If you wish a complete list of our books please ask at your local library or write directly to:

Dales Large Print Books
Magna House, Long Preston,
Skipton, North Yorkshire.
BD23 4ND

This Large Print Book, for people
who cannot read normal print,
is published under the auspices of

THE ULVERSCROFT FOUNDATION